INFINITE

A Gift Changes Everything

INFINITE

A Gift Changes Everything

T. C. Steuer

Steuer Management, LLC

Alpine, Utah

T. C. Steuer

Steuer Management

Alpine, Utah

www.tcsteuer.com

Publisher's Note: This is a work of fiction. Names, characters, places, and incidents are a product of the author's imagination. Locales and public names are sometimes used for atmospheric purposes. Any resemblance to actual people, living or dead, or to businesses, companies, events, institutions, or locales is completely coincidental.

Book Layout © 2018 BookDesignTemplates.com

Infinite / T. C. Steuer. -- 1st ed.

ISBN 978-0-9993337-2-3

This book is dedicated to

My friends who inspired me,
my family for their never-ending support,
and to my mom who taught me that no matter what
"have courage and be kind" - Cinderella.

Contents

The Party 1

Secrets...20

An Impossible Reality 28

Eighteen Today—Now I Can Buy Some Dry Ice.............45

Listen 60

Pole Hill...74

The Sky Is Green..93

Wanted 109

Lost and Found 117

Pie in the Sky...133

Interrogated 146

Cumberland 159

At the End of the Tunnel Is a Train 164

A Mother Knows 173

A Love Betrayed 178

The Bond 197

Extraction 211

Time Is the Measure of Change 225

INFINITE

A Gift Changes Everything

The Party

WHEN I WAS THREE YEARS OLD my mother walked out the door and never looked back. I don't remember her. I have a photograph from before she left that puts a face to a name, but that's it. I used to hold out hope that she would come back for me someday. I know better now.

I stopped asking questions about her a long time ago because my dad never answered. It hurt him too much. He's still in love with her. And no matter what I say, he won't move on. He still thinks she's coming back because that's what she told me in her letter.

Dear Paris,

I'm so sorry. There is no excuse. But I want you to know how much I love you. You mean everything to me. I want to be there for you, always and forever, but the only way for you to truly live a normal life, a life full of happiness and safety, is for me to not be a part of it. And that breaks my heart. I have failed as a mother. I failed to keep you safe, but without me you might have a chance. I know this may sound crazy now, but one day you will understand.

My love for you stretches infinitely, beyond all obstacles, just like your knowledge will soon do. I hope that someday you will be able to forgive me and that we can be together again. I love you.

With all my heart,

Mom

If she loved me, then why leave? Didn't her walking out on me automatically make it impossible for me to live a normal life? And how did she fail to keep me safe? I'm here alive and well.

Regardless, I'm done waiting for her. I've wasted fifteen years holding out hope. But now I accept that she left me and my dad to fend on our own. So no. I'm not going to wait for the day when she comes knocking on my door. Life with just me and my dad is pretty amazing and I wouldn't have it any other way. He learned how to do hair, took me shopping, listened to all my ramblings, and he even bought me my first eye shadow palette—hot pink and sparkles (a valiant effort).

It was just the two of us, always on the road in our tiny one-bedroom camper. There was nothing we hadn't seen, nowhere we hadn't visited in the States...well, at least the places that matter. I thought we were going to travel the world, continuing Maverick and Paris's Taylor tales (my dads attempt at wordplay that somehow stuck since our last name is Taylor), but three years ago my dad suddenly sold the camper and bought a house in small town Alpine, Utah. "It's time for you to make some friends," he said.

But I didn't want to make friends. I was happy with just me and my dad. We'd made so many good memories, like when I was ten and we found ourselves in Long Beach, California, where my dad decided that Walmart's parking lot would be a good home. We spent two months learning to surf, going to movie premieres, and riding every ride at Disneyland twice. When we were ready for a change, we packed up and drove to Tennessee where I learned how to fight, hunt, hock a loogie, and stay on one of those mechanical bulls for a solid eight seconds. I had everything I ever wanted. Just me and my dad, two best friends going on crazy adventures and living life to the fullest.

When I walked into Lone Peak High School it was my first day of school, ever. I was a sophomore and one out of 2,876 kids. I had decided to take it one day at a time, just like I always do, with confidence and positivity—the two principles that my dad drilled into me as a child. But that didn't work.

At first I didn't know how to talk to people because I had never been anywhere long enough to make a friend before. I tried smiling at people in the halls, talking to strangers in my classes, and approaching groups at lunch, but it didn't make a difference. Eventually school became a chore. A sad chore where I ate my lunch in the bathroom stall or the little square corner in the 800 hall.

One day I found a group I could potentially call my friends. I was ecstatic until I realized that no matter what I did or said, if I didn't send the first text inviting myself to tag along for whatever activity they were doing that night then I wasn't invited. Not one of them ever texted me, called me, or reached out in any way. And those times when I mustered up all my courage to invite myself, it was clear that they were just tolerating me out of pity. After months of trying, it wasn't worth it anymore.

Just when I was about to give up, I met a girl named Emily Chase. We were sat together in a new seating chart in fourth period English with Ms. Miller—more commonly known as Ms. Satan—and we have been best friends ever since. Miracles really do happen.

Emily—or as her friends call her, Em—instantly pulled me into her life. She introduced me to her best friend at the time, Bentley, and the three of us became inseparable. They taught me everything that I needed to know about high school. They kept me updated on new fashion trends and taught me how to flirt, socialize, walk in heels, and they even gave me a nickname: Par, which sounds like "Pear." It's short for Paris.

I never knew just how amazing friends could be. They can change your life.

For a while the three of us were happy, but then it was just Em and me. Not out of choice—there was nothing we could do about it. Bentley was gone. And we were different. A good different.

"Paris, come on!"

Startled, I slightly turn my head from the poster of a young mother and daughter that's hanging on the wall of the grocery store to face Em. "Sorry, just got lost in thought, I guess."

"Well, let's go let's go let's go let's go," Em sings. She takes off running toward the checkout stand. Luckily I have long legs to match hers or I would never be able to keep up.

I used to idolize Em. Her flawless beauty, thin legs, and thick long brown hair—a cheerleader, of course. Strangers bow down at her feet and she doesn't see it. She's the sweetest, most down-to-earth girl I've ever met and everyone loves her for it.

I'm surprised that Em and my friendship has lasted this long. We're polar opposites. She likes pop, I like country. She likes chick flicks, I like action. She likes fashion, I like thrift stores. The only thing we have ever agreed on is to agree to disagree. Our three favorite words.

"Paris," Em says, sliding away from the counter.

"What?" I ask.

"That will be $53.77. Credit or debit?" the cashier asks, towering over me. He has to be at least 6'4" because I'm not short.

Oh, I see. Classic Em. "Debit." I hand the boy my card. "You know, I'm going to go broke if I don't drop you as a friend soon, Em."

"I didn't think 'broke' existed in your vocabulary. Besides, if we're not friends then who's going to tell you when it's been an appropriate amount of time after Memorial Day to wear white pants? Or that your outfit reminds me of a Southern second-grader's."

"Ha ha, you're so funny." Okay, fine, that may be true.

"You guys having some kind of girls' night?" the cashier asks, nodding at our bags filled with chips and soda.

Why is he staring at me? And what is he doing with his gorgeous blonde hair? Stop touching it, you're messing up the style.

"Uh, no, a party," I say. "It's our Friday tradition. Em hosts and buys pizza. I supply the rest."

"Got it," he says. He bends forward, placing his elbow on the counter, then ever so slowly rests his chin in the palm of one hand and my receipt in the other. A faint smile grows—his sexy face, I can tell, and he's good at it. "So she's Em—" he gestures with his eyes— "and you are?"

"Taken," I say while ripping the receipt from his hand.

"This is Paris," Em says as she grabs the receipt from me. She scribbles something down on the bottom of the receipt while I pick up the bags of junk food.

"Lets go," I say. I link arms with Em and pull her toward the exit.

"That's her number and the address for the party tonight," she calls out.

"No," I say as I attempt to cover her mouth.

"See you at nine," Em shouts as she shakes free.

I'm going to kill her. "Em!" I chase after her in the parking lot. "We don't even know his name."

"Who cares. He was hot and he was into you," she says while climbing into the driver's seat of her brand-new white Jeep Wrangler. I throw the groceries in the back and join her in the passenger seat.

"He was not into me."

"Are you kidding? He couldn't have been more obvious. When are you going to realize how beautiful you are? Boys can't take their eyes off of you."

"Oh, whatever."

"No, it's true. I'm sick of you not realizing how freaking gorgeous you are. Look at you. You have this long thick perfect hair that's sun-kissed blonde, a toned slim figure without ever going to the gym, a sexy fashion style— thanks to me—and never-ending legs. You look like the child of Blake Lively and Julianne Hough."

"Julianne Hough…"

"From Safe Haven."

"That's right," I say. "Well you're even prettier."

"This isn't a competition. We're both beautiful."

I reach across the car and hug her. Somehow she always knows exactly what to say.

"Get off of me," she says. "You're going to make me crash."

"I love you, Em."

"I love you too."

"But I still can't believe you gave a stranger my number! You know I love Camden. Besides, what if he turns out to be a serial killer?"

Em snorts. "Really?"

"What, it could happen." I say.

"In a movie maybe. Plus, if you and Camden ever break up, now you have the perfect rebound."

"I don't think Camden and I are ever going to break up."

"Yeah, I know you guys are perfect together and blah, blah, blah."

"Better than perfect," I say.

Em blasts the music so loud that the car is shaking.

"Hey!" I shout as I turn it down. "We still need to figure out who you're the child of. I'm thinking maybe Lily Collins and Nina Dobrev, but with a little lighter hair."

Em laughs. "I wish."

"I thought that was pretty close."

Em rolls her eyes and turns up the music. "I Knew You Were Trouble" by Taylor Swift pounds in my ear.

Camden wasn't trouble. Neither of us planned on falling in love, but it just kind of happened.

About a year ago, at the end of my junior year, a new kid moved to town. I hadn't met him, but I heard rumors. Lots and lots of them from girls with virgin lips. According to the VLs, he had a boxy face with a sharp cut jaw, irresistible lips, deep blue eyes, and when he looked at you he slightly lifted one eyebrow. Not a single girl had survived that look without falling madly in love.

Within a week his hair was the talk of the school. It was a sun-kissed blonde color like mine. He trimmed the sides short and let the top go wild. He never used product, yet somehow it always stayed perfect.

The first time I ever met Camden I was walking in the halls with a boy after my AP Chemistry class, Tyson. He was arguably one of the smartest kids in the school, yet sadly people couldn't see past his geeky exterior to the funny kid inside. Shad, the captain of the football team, approached us to ask me to lunch. I said no. "I'll just take out the trash then," Shad said and slammed Tyson against the lockers.

Before I had a chance to even yell at him, Camden grabbed Shad by the shirt and threw him to the ground. I rushed to help Tyson up. In front of Shad I asked Tyson if he would like to go to lunch with me, and he said yes. We thanked Camden and headed for the cafeteria. If I'm being honest I didn't think that people like Camden existed. Also, the rumors about his appearance did not do him justice.

I didn't see Camden again until the following Friday night at one of Em and my parties. A group of kids who had a lot too much to drink decided to crash the party. Camden once again came to the rescue and attempted to kick them out. Meanwhile one of the boys—Dawson, a drop out from my AP Statistics class—came onto me very strongly and wouldn't let go. His breath reeked of overripe fruit and ethanol-based hand sanitizer. Before Camden could rip Dawson off, I kneed him in the crotch and punched him in the face. Dawson got the message loud and clear and left with the rest of his gang.

Things just took off with Camden that night. It was completely illogical yet spontaneous, and we couldn't help it. He took me on dates almost every week. By the end of the month we were dating and have been ever since. He's perfect in every way—well, except that he can be pretty possessive of me. I can take care of myself, thank you very much. But his body...ugh, he's strong, incredibly strong, like mind-altering strong, and not too big like some guys whose arms are the size of my thigh. No, Camden's like a young Paul Walker with a smaller forehead and a prettier face—I didn't think it was possible either. He's also fashionable, always wearing jeans or khakis with nice denim or button-up shirts.

"Let's go," Em says.

"What?"

"Again?"

"Sorry, I know, I can't help it," I say. "I mentioned Camden and then my thoughts just drifted."

"Well, Mrs. Freeman, would you be so kind as to help me carry this stuff into the house?" Em asks in a proper English accent. "The party's starting in like ten minutes."

"I would be delighted to," I say, mimicking her. "Mrs. Freeman? Don't you think that's a little premature? Although Paris Freeman does have a nice ring to it."

"Come on, we both know you guys are getting married."

I can't stop grinning as Em and I unload the car and set up for the party. Out of the corner of my eye I spot Camden walking toward me. Em has made it very clear to the school that she has an open-door policy. If you knock, she won't come—you just have to walk in.

"Hey!" Camden says as he gently grabs me and in the most romantic way, placing his luscious lips on mine.

"Hey," I manage to say back after our kiss. I just about died; it's amazing how that never gets old. I didn't want him to stop. "Congrats on your game. You played amazing."

"Thank you. I thought for sure Coach wasn't going to let me play after missing practice."

"Lacrosse is in your blood—Coach would be stupid not to play you."

Camden takes a deep breath and just stares at me.

"Do I have something in my teeth?" I ask.

"No."

"Well, what is it then? A giant zit?" I ask while feeling my face.

"No, your skin is flawless," Camden says.

"Then what?"

"I've never seen someone so beautiful in my life."

My cheeks turn hot. "You're not so bad yourself."

"Oh, get a room," Em says.

"Okay," Camden says, swiping me off my feet and throwing me over his shoulder then sprinting toward the stairs.

I scream with laughter as I shout at him to put me down.

"Hey, not my room!" Em says. "Actually, I think we left the drinks in the back of the car. Will you guys please go get them?" Camden sets me back down. "Thank you. And hurry—people will be here soon."

I'm reaching for the handle of the car door when I feel two hands wrap around my waist. Camden picks me up, pulling me away from the door. I shout through laughter, hitting his arms in an attempt to break free.

"Man, you just can't keep your hands off of me today, can you?"

"You want me to stop?" he asks.

"I didn't say that." I twist around in his arms. He looks at me with a huge smile. He leans in to kiss me, and his sexy lips take my heart on a rollercoaster ride. He slowly loosens his grip and I slide down his chest till my feet are touching the ground. I push him off me and open the car door.

"Em said to hurry, remember? People are going to be here soon."

"Come on, just a little longer," he says.

I roll my eyes and shove two bottles of soda into his hands. As I reach back into the car, something hits me fast. I don't feel so great. I don't know what it is, but something's wrong with me. I've never felt this way before. I rush back inside and toward the bathroom as Camden chases after me, asking what's wrong. I slam the bathroom door behind me and hover over the toilet. I don't think I'm going to throw up but I don't know what else it could be.

I hear a knock at the door. Em slowly opens the door and crouches at my side. I can tell that she's as confused as me because she's giving me her "what the crap" face. I'm not sure if I'm going to pass out, throw up, or what. I stand back up and lean against the wall. I've been sick before, badly sick, in the hospital sick, and this is nothing like it.

"Are you pregnant?" she asks. "You're pregnant aren't you?"

"That's not funny, you know that I'm waiting till I get married." I groan. All of a sudden everything rushes to my head and I feel like I'm about to pass out, I'm engulfed by pulsing lights. I can't feel my feet. Everything is tingling.

"Em, I don't feel so good…"

∞   ∞   ∞

A colorful lab room with pink and yellow walls appears in front of me. Cabinets and tables line the walls. All of the cabinet tops are covered in different complicated looking equipment. Two couches and a comfy chair sit across from the door, forming their own living room of sorts.

A woman in a white lab coat with a bright pink dress poking out from the bottom stands next to the only monotone thing in the room: a large—no, huge—glass and metal capsule, twelve feet tall and wide enough to fit an extremely large man within it, stood in the center of the lab. It's the only thing not pressed up against the walls. Wires hang from all over. The word GIFT is taped across the clear glass on the front of the capsule. The more I look at it, the more it reminds me of a modern looking spray-tanning booth.

I make a full loop around the lab, looking at the things that the woman is working on—chemical compounds, parts of meteors, and random things from deep in the ocean. There's a bunch of other stuff that I don't understand—maybe I should have paid more attention in chemistry.

Everything in the lab looks like it's from another time. The colors and fun of the 1980s but the science of 2050. The woman looks in my direction but doesn't seem to notice me.

Blueprints for the Gift hang on the wall. The blueprints don't say anything about what it does; there's only schematics and numbers. However, one thing stands out in the blueprints—a person standing inside the Gift.

Curious, I walk across the lab to the woman in pink and tilt my head toward the blueprints. This giant spray-tanning booth is designed to test all sorts of chemical solutions on people.

Immediately I blurt out... "Is this legal?" The woman doesn't respond. "Cause, I mean, human testing? You don't look like that type of woman—an evil mad scientist. I really hope you aren't one."

Still no response whatsoever from the woman. Not even a nonverbal acknowledgement that I have spoken. Confused, I try to tap the woman in pink on the shoulder. My hand goes right through her.

Is this a dream? A vision or hallucination? A hologram?

A dream, I decide. And I am done with it. I poke and pinch myself, then slap my face. But I can't wake up. For what seems like hours, the woman continues to do random things around the lab while I watch.

As even more time slowly ticks by I'm starting to get irritated. I try to pick up a beaker and smash it to the ground, but my hand goes straight through it. I've never had a dream like this—being a ghost that couldn't touch things.

At the end of the day the woman takes off her white lab jacket and hangs it on the rack by the door. As she puts on a large winter jacket I shout at her, anxious to get out of there. When the woman opens the door, I decide to follow her. Maybe leaving the lab might trigger something, causing me to wake up. But as I reach the door I freeze. Something is blocking me from leaving the lab. I take a step back and try to break through the window next to the door. Nope. Still stuck.

Since I seem to have all the time in the world, I look out the window, curious to see if I can tell where I am. There is nothing but darkness. With a sinking feeling I resign myself to waiting for whatever is going to happen. I walk to the couches while checking my phone. I have no service, but the screen reads 9:04 P.M. Would I be able to sleep? Can you sleep in a dream? I laugh to myself—this is like the movie Inception. A dream within a dream within a dream.

Before I can lay my head down, light breaks through the window, filling the lab with sunshine. I look at my phone again. Now it reads 8:04 A.M. Did someone press a fast-forward button? Maybe I did fall asleep in my dream? Maybe this isn't a dream at all?

I get up and peer through the window. The building is stretched out alongside the ocean. Giant waves crash up against the concrete. Beautiful dark blue water crackles in the light.

I hear a loud squeaking noise followed by tears. I whirl around to see that the woman has returned. This time her dress is yellow and she's not alone. She's carrying a toddler who is the source of the tears. The little girl has long blond hair that's pulled back into two perfect pigtails. She's wearing a pink shirt with blue jean overalls. The woman in yellow places the girl on the ground and tells her to stay put. Her tears turn into a tantrum. The woman picks the child back up and rocks her until the crying stops. Then she walks her over to the couches and sets her down with a bag of toys. The woman puts on her white lab coat and resumes her work, constantly looking over her shoulder to make sure the little girl is okay.

Hours pass of the same routine. The woman would do a little work while the toddler crawls around and plays with her toys. Then the little girl finds a stepstool pressed against a counter and starts to climb it. I'm a little alarmed. Why would the woman bring a toddler to a dangerous lab? I reach for the little girl and of course my hand goes right through her. I watch the toddler crawl across the counter toward the row of colorful buttons. Ones that you would expect any toddler to push.

The woman's head turns sharply when she hears the crash of her tools falling to the ground. She races to get the toddler and places her back on the couch. After comforting the child the woman begins to gather her fallen tools. The toddler, now free of the woman's grasp, quickly crawls away in search of a new form of entertainment. She totters straight for a giant red button on the Gift that might as well spell out doom.

Unable to touch anything, say anything, or connect in any way possible, I sit down on the couch and wait. Waiting for some tragedy to happen. Waiting for my dream to end. Waiting to see my friends and father again.

The toddler reaches for the button on the Gift. Her tiny fingers manage to skim the edge. She pushes it.

Nothing happens and I have to laugh. Then the woman screams. A white mist begins to flow into the Gift. With the door of the Gift wide open, the mist rapidly fills the room. As the woman runs to her crying toddler, they both breathe in the mist and drop to the floor unconscious.

Their faces turn hot pink. Then their skin begins to boil. A gruesome stream of blood flows from their noses. I cover my mouth in horror. I just watched two people die right in front of me. What kind of dream was this?

I bury my face in my arm and cry. When I look up, the bodies are shaking as if they're having a seizure. Then they fall still.

I don't want to look at their lifeless bodies, but I can't help myself. I search for any sign in their expressions that might mean they're still alive. A slight twitch from the toddler's hand catches my eye. Then a more distinct movement on her mother's face. Her eyelids flutter slowly at first then she stands straight up as if nothing had even happened. I'm pretty sure that I'm watching a ghost. Will the woman be able to see me now?

After the woman gains her footing, her emotions begin to change rapidly. At first she looks worried. Then confused. Then terrified. Finally, excitement brightens her face.

When her hand touches the toddler's shoulder, their bodies begin to seize again. When the screaming finally ends, both the woman and the girl lie silent and breathless, sprawled out on the floor. The woman starts to cry. After a moment she walks to the cabinets and pulls out a towel. When she starts to wrap it around the girl, they instantly start convulsing and screaming again. I close my eyes, cover my ears, and cry.

Secrets

I SEE A BRIGHT LIGHT shining from above me. Am I dead? Am I dying? Oh wait, it's the ceiling fixture. Em, my dad, and Camden are standing above me. "What happened?"

"Well," Em begins, "what's the last thing you remember and I'll go from there."

"Falling down."

She smiles. "There's a lot you need to hear then. Get comfy. Your face turned bright red and you passed out. I called to Camden, who was waiting by the door."

Why did she have to get Camden involved? I don't want him to see me like this.

"I ran in and you were, well, passed out on the floor," Camden says.

"Yeah, you passed out in my arms," Em says. "Although I'm not so sure that passed out is the right description because you started shaking."

Shaking? What the crap does that mean?

"You were turning and tossing on the floor. I kept trying to wake you, but I didn't want to do anything that would hurt you. I didn't know what to do. I thought about calling an ambulance, but you probably would have killed me after what happened the last time."

I laughed. "Smart call. That would have been another nightmare within a nightmare or whatever you call what happened to me."

"Yeah, but Paris, it looked like you were having some kind of seizure," Em says. "Don't do that again!"

"I don't think I can control it, sorry," I say with a smile.

"It's not funny, you scared me to death. Anyways, Camden carried you to my car and we drove you home. We thought that would be the best place for you." Em looks at my dad. "Camden, we should probably go and let her rest." Em bends down to the bed and gives me the biggest hug.

"Yeah, okay," Camden says, a little reluctantly. "I hope you feel better." He kisses me goodbye.

My dad walks them out while I lie in bed. I can hear faint whispering—they're talking about something but I can't make out the words. The door slams shut, separating me from my friends. Leaving me with only my dad, just like old times.

"Dad?"

"Be right there!" he shouts back. I hear footsteps down the hall. My door begins to open, but then it quickly slams back closed and my dad knocks three times.

"You remembered to knock! Come in," I manage to say through my laughter. He sits on my bed next to me.

"Do you know what's happening to me?" I ask.

"I do," he says.

"Wait, what? You do?"

"Sweetie, there's something I've been keeping from you. I wanted to tell you a long time ago, but your mom thought it would be best if I waited."

My mom? Why does she get a say? Why is he listening to her in the first place? She left us.

"Until you started showing signs," he adds. He sighs. "I want you to know when your mother first told me this, I thought she was a little insane, but it's true. All of it."

"What's true?" I ask.

"Here it goes—no more secrets and no more lies. Well, your mother was one of the most brilliant scientists I'd ever met. She wasn't an ordinary scientist—she specialized in biology, neurobiology, geology, and meteorology. She was particularly interested in opening up our ability to use more than five percent of our brains."

"But that's not possible."

"At the time it wasn't," he says.

"At the time?"

"Fifteen and a half years ago, when you were almost three, your mom was trying to find a way to augment human brains. She worked in secret for years, trying to protect her research from the USI."

"USI?"

"Unknown Secret Intelligence. It's a secret federal agency that deals with new threats and technology that could potentially be dangerous."

"But why would the government hurt someone who's trying to make people smarter?"

"Not everything is always so black and white."

"Is that your subtle way of saying that the USI would hurt us?"

"Well if it came to that, yes. The USI will do anything they can to protect lives. Anything."

"Will they kill us?"

"If they thought killing us would save others."

"But why? We didn't do anything."

"You won't remember this, but all those years ago the babysitter canceled on us last minute. I had a very important board meeting regarding the construction plans for the children's hospital where I used to work. Since there was no way I could bring you with me, your mom was forced to take you. I convinced her that it would be fine. I was wrong."

"Please," I say. "Just tell me what happened."

"Your mother had created a chemical formula that would potentially "open up minds," as she would often say. Though she didn't know if the experiment would work— and if it did, how effective it would be. No trials had been conducted yet. Your mother and her assistant had built a diffuser large enough to fit a fully grown man inside. Your mom was modifying it for her new project. She was planning to test a brand-new formula the day she brought you in, but when the sitter canceled she decided to postpone the first trial."

This is starting to feel terribly familiar…Edges of my dream from while I was passed out start to creep back into my mind.

"She didn't know that her lab assistant had already loaded the new formula into the diffuser. While she was working the diffuser activated and you were both exposed to the chemical."

"So what's going to happen to me?" I whisper. "Am I going to die?"

"No," my dad says. "You're going to get smarter."

I don't believe it. I can't believe it. But then how could I have this memory?

"Nikki tried to get you out, but she couldn't touch you without causing you both to have excruciating seizures. When the USI learned of her research she had no choice but to leave. That's why I never moved on. I still love her, and she's still out there, loving me."

So the little girl in my dream, that was me. It was real. It wasn't a dream, it was a memory. A weird one from some other perspective, but still a memory.

Should I tell my dad that I believe him? What if I change my mind? What if there's another reason and my dad's just insane? I don't know … No, I do know. I know it's true. And I want it to be true. My mom didn't leave because she didn't love us.

I finally understand what she meant by "The only way for you to truly live a normal life and be safe is for me to not be a part of it" in her letter. That means she might—might—still love me. She might be worth finding. If the day ever comes when we won't hurt each other.

Maybe I was too quick to give up hope. Maybe this is the time she was talking about. Maybe she's coming home.

I feel a huge stab of guilt. By pressing that button I tore my parents from each other.

"Dad, I'm so sorry," I say. "I'm sorry I pressed that button."

His eyebrows rise. "You remember that?" He takes my hand. "Paris, you were two years old. No one can blame a two-year-old for being curious."

I shut my eyes, squeezing out a pair of tears. "How can you know she's still the same person?" I ask after a moment. How would he know that she hasn't found someone else and simply moved on?

"Paris, you don't understand. She's the one. She always has and always will be the one. If she learns how to fix this she will. She's going to come home." A large grin stretches across his face.

"But how can she come home? She doesn't know where to find us."

"I thought the same thing but when I asked her she said, 'I can't explain it so you're just going to have to trust me.' And I do."

That doesn't make any sense—then again, nothing does. As much as I want her to come home, she'll never find us. Actually, you know what? I don't want her to find us. I went this long without a mom—I don't need her. And if she comes back and can't stay with us, that would kill me. I can't lose her again.

Even if she never comes home, I hope that she'll never stop loving us. I hope she never forgets that I'm her daughter or that she's still married to my dad. She's still my mom, and Dad still loves her.

Dad tucks a strand of hair behind my ear. "Nikki thought you might grow into your mind, and I guess you're starting to now."

I'm growing into my mind? Does that mean she can come home? I climb out of bed and circle the room like a vulture, rubbing my hands up and down my thighs, my head hung low. I take two deep breaths then stop in front of my bathroom mirror.

How could this be my life? I'm just an ordinary teenage girl.

I rub my eyes twice. My hands slide down my face to the back of my neck then to my mouth. My breathing accelerates as I fixate on myself in the mirror.

"I know this sounds crazy," my dad says from my bedroom. "Take your time and think it over."

I don't respond. Think about it? I can't stop thinking about it. Was Mom crazy? Or was she telling the impossible truth? Even with the dream or memory—

whatever it is—it's not possible. This kind of stuff doesn't happen in real life.

"Things are going to start changing for you soon," he adds. "Your mind will begin to do more."

My eyes drift from my own to his in the mirror. "What do you mean?" I ask.

"Eventually your mind is going to be able to do amazing things."

"Like, what? I'm gonna have superpowers? That's just insane."

"Not superpowers, a gift. The ultimate gift."

"More like the ultimate curse," I say, "if it's even true. Which..." I take a long pause then turn to face him. "Wait...what could you even do with an 'augmented' brain?"

"Let's not worry about that today."

"Dad, I want to know."

"Honestly, I don't know exactly. Only your mother would know. And, Paris, you can't tell anyone about any of this. Not Em, not Camden, no one. Understood?"

"What? Why? They deserve to know!"

"Paris, the USI is dangerous. If word gets out and they hear about it, they might come for you. I can't lose you and your mother. Please, promise me you won't say anything."

His face is pale, and sweat has beaded up on his forehead. He's never this dead set on something. And never, ever this serious.

"Okay. I promise I won't tell anyone."

CHAPTER 3

An Impossible Reality

MAVERICK HAD BEEN DREADING that moment since the day Nikki came home from the lab with Paris. As a father he felt like he had failed his daughter. As a husband he felt like he failed his wife. He knew that Nikki's work was unsafe. Yes, there had never been a problem in the lab before, but no one had ever brought a toddler into the lab.

Rick changed out of his Oxford button-down and into his ragged robe. He brushed his teeth, then grabbed the remote and hopped into bed. He flipped through channel after channel, nothing capturing his attention. He turned the TV off, fixed his pillows, and stared at the blank white ceiling. He remembered every second of that awful day. September 26, 2002, the last day he would see his wife.

∞   ∞   ∞

I grab my coat, eager to get home. Make no mistake, I love the hospital, but I hate that I can't be home more.

I pull the car into the double garage, which has become a single because of the clutter that's piled up over the years. Safes full of weapons, boxes of old toys, clothes, and of course mountains of Nikki's research, all piled into the right half.

The house is empty so I decide to start dinner. I open the fridge, looking for inspiration. I don't do much cooking because I'm not very good and Nikki loves it. There's a package of ground beef in the freezer and eggs and spinach in the fridge. Salad and spaghetti with meatballs it is. I also throw some cookie dough we had left over from the other night into the oven for desert.

As I'm rolling the meatballs I start to grow concerned. Where are they? Nikki's always home before seven, always. By nine o'clock I've turned off the heat under the tomato sauce, put the meatballs back in the fridge, and am sitting at the kitchen counter with clammy hands. There's nothing I can do—I don't have a number for the lab and I'm not even allowed to enter the building. Car problems? Traffic? I clamp my teeth together trying to squish the next thought. What if the USI took her? And if they did, what did they do to Paris?

I'm near the edge of panic when it hits me—there is one way that I can put my mind at ease about the USI.

Ryker. I pick up the phone and dial his number.

No answer. I call again. On my third try he picks up.

"Hello?"

"Ryker, it's Rick. I need your help."

"Rick? Rick who?"

"What are you talking about? It's me, Rick Taylor. I need to know if the USI has locked on to our location or not. Are we still safe?"

"Sorry, Rick. My mind went blank there for a second. No the USI hasn't locked on. You're still safe."

There's something in his voice that strikes me as off. "Ryker? Have you been compromised?"

"No," he says quickly.

This isn't him. Something's wrong. "What did I say to you the night I left?"

A long pause follows. "You think you're so smart, don't you?" a strange voice cuts in saying.

"What did you do to him?" I ask.

"Ryker's fine, calm down. This little stunt you pulled— very smart, but it's over."

"Terrence? Terrence, is that you?" I ask.

"It's been a long time, Rick. How's the baby? Paris, is it?"

"Son of a—" I slam the phone down on the table.

That was a mistake. They've surely tracked my call, so we need to get out of here. They're closest ground unit would be in New York—that gives us roughly five hours. We need to be out of here by two A.M. Where is Nikki?

I rush upstairs and begin packing. We don't need to bring anything—we have millions of dollars between us— but I want as much as I can from this place because it's all such happy memories. It's a simple little house—what's the point of buying something gaudy when you're trying to blend in—but it's everything that Nikki ever dreamed of. Each room painted a different bright color, a picket fence, a beautiful lawn that leads to a forest of spruce trees out back.

I glance down at my watch again: one A.M. Where could they be? If we don't leave soon, we won't make it out of here.

Everything's packed but food from the kitchen. I pull out a large blue cooler from the garage, line the bottom with ice, and stuff it full of everything perishable.

The front door opens. I drop a container of grapes and press my back up against the wall. I grab the gun that's tucked into the back of my pants and level it toward Nikki? Or the USI?

"Nikki? Nikki is that you?"

I'm answered only by her sobs. I step into the hallway, where Nikki stands with her head bent, her face cloaked by the hood that's soaked from the pouring rain.

"I'm...I'm so, so sorry," she says.

"Nikki!" I tuck the gun away and run toward her.

"No! No! Stay back! Please stay back!" she says, burying herself in the corner, her back to me.

"What? What's going on?" I ask. "Did I do something?"

"No," she says, frantically shaking her head. She slowly falls to the ground, pulling her legs into a little ball.

I take a deep breath to recollect myself. "Honey, please —"

"Stay back!" she shouts.

"Okay, okay. I'm sorry." I say, raising my hands and taking a step back. "But please, tell me."

"I have a lot to tell you—I just have to find the words." She starts to cry again. "But it's going to end with you and Paris leaving town and me disappearing until it's safe."

"What? That's not happening. I'll never leave you!"

"You're not leaving me...I am. I made a terrible mistake, and I can't stay here. Neither can you."

Nikki dives straight into the story of what happened, sparing no details. I want to comfort her, but she's scared to touch me.

"So where is Paris? How did you get home?" I ask.

"I can't ever hold my daughter in my arms again," she sobs. "Ever. I can't braid her hair, dress her for her first day of school, comfort her when she's had a bad day ..." Her eyes are bloodshot and snot drips from her nose. "I don't know anything about it. I don't know if it will happen if I touch you."

"I can handle the pain. I just want to hold you in my arms again. Please let me do that for you."

"You don't understand. No one should ever have to endure this pain. And even if you could, I can't. Not again. I can still feel it now, a burning in my head. Each time I touched her it got worse."

"I don't know what to say..."

"I know. There's nothing you can say. I made Paris walk all the way to the car. By the end she was crawling, she was so shattered from the pain." Nikki sits against the wall and rubs at the mascara smeared on her face. "I don't know anything about what's happening. We hadn't done any testing yet. We have no idea if this is the correct formula. What if something worse happens? I might have killed my own daughter."

"Sweetie, none of this is your fault," I say. "I'm the one who made you bring her to work."

"If I had just watched her a little more carefully nothing would have happened."

I reach for her hand. "You don't know that—"

"No!" Nikki shouts, but I grab her hand anyway. Nothing happens. No pain, no screaming, everything's okay. I sit down next to her and she relaxes into my arms.

"You're going to take Paris and get out of here," she says. "Keep her hidden. If my chemical compounds were added correctly, she has the Gift now. She may be the key to everything."

I stare at Nikki, trying to memorize her beautiful face. "And what about you?" I ask.

"I'm going to learn how to control this, how to stop it, so that I can come back."

"Nikki…When you didn't come home, I called Ryker. I thought maybe the USI had found us somehow. They didn't, but Ryker's compromised."

Nikki leaps to her feet. "What? We need to get out of here! You take the minivan, I'll take the BMW."

I embrace her, unwilling to let her leave. "This can't be goodbye," I whisper. Her soaking long brown hair sticks to my cheek.

"Rick, we don't have a choice," she says, pulling away. "We have to think logically here. We can stay in the Marriott in Cambridge tonight, get burner phones tomorrow, and—"

With a crash canisters of nerve gas break through the front windows.

"Run!" Nikki shouts. She hands me the keys to the minivan and I pull my gun. I burst out the front door, firing wildly as I run forward in a crouch. The agents can't risk shooting back and I'm able to duck into the minivan. They've blocked the end of the driveway so I drive through the front lawn and bounce over the curb. One car follows me but I manage to shake it by shooting out its wheels.

An hour later I stop to make one last call on my cell. Nikki doesn't answer. After a long moment where my heart almost breaks in despair, I toss the phone into the lake.

∞   ∞   ∞

I knock on my dad's door.

"Yes?"

I crack the door and peek my head in. "Dad, it's almost one in the afternoon."

"Yeah, I had a bit of a long night. It's Saturday, right?"

"Um no, Sunday. We missed church."

"Paris, I think it might be best for you to stay home for awhile. At least until the seizures stop."

"How long is a while?" I ask.

"I'm not sure."

I shrug then close the door behind me. No school then. Okay.

As I walk away I hear a faint whisper coming from my dad's room. Who is he talking to? I tiptoe back to his door and place my ear against the door.

"She made it. She made it," he whispers.

I think he's going insane. I don't know what his problem is, but I should be the one who's losing it. I'm the one who just found out I was a lab rat as a baby.

∞   ∞   ∞

It's been eleven days of house arrest. My dad and I haven't talked about what happened since the first time. And as much as I love my dad, I don't think I can survive another day without going to school. I've missed almost two weeks but I keep having episodes. I drop to the floor unconscious and shake like I'm having an epileptic seizure. They're totally random, so I can't prepare for them. I'll have an episode three or four times in the same day, or none at all. I spend all my time in bed sleeping yet I'm always exhausted.

I want to see my friends but my dad won't let them visit. It makes no sense—first he moves me here and forces me to make friends and now he won't let me anywhere near them. I know, I know, we have to keep what's happening to me a secret or the USI will come and blah, blah, blah. But Em and Camden were the first ones to watch one of my episodes. They already know that something's up.

I bet they're freaking out. They probably think I'm dead. My dad took my phone away, and my laptop. This is exactly how I imagine prison to be, except that I don't have to wear those hideous jumpsuits.

He says that I wouldn't want my friends to see me in pain, but it's more painful going through this without them. Em and I are sisters—no, we're closer than sisters. And Camden, he makes me happy, he makes laugh. With the two of them here I think my episodes wouldn't hurt as bad. After every episode I wake up with a searing pain in my head that gets worse and worse each time, and I need my friends' support.

A slam of the front door echoes through the house. Dad? Why would he be up this early? I slide my feet out of bed while holding my head then inch my way to the top of the stairs. Wincing, I shuffle down the stairs and join my dad in the kitchen. He's pulling some gross takeout leftovers out of the fridge from dinner the night before. But wow, he looks good today. Dressed all fancy in his tailored suit, his black hair combed back.

"Chinese for breakfast again," I say, hunching over and faking a dry heave.

"Nope, just throwing it away. I was thinking maybe some crepes this morning."

I lift my eyebrows, "What's the occasion?"

"Does there have to be an occasion for me to make my beautiful daughter a nice breakfast for once?" he asks.

"No, but there does have to be an occasion for you to be in that suit, so spill."

He takes a deep breath. "One, it's your birthday tomorrow and two, it's our anniversary. Twenty-three years."

I rush straight for him, and he wraps his arms around me in a giant bear hug. "I love you," I say.

"I love you too," he says kissing my forehead. "And that's why I'm doing all of this. I know you're upset that you can't see your friends, but I lost your mother and I'm not going to lose you too."

"Nothing's going to happen to me."

"Your optimism astounds me. You get that from your mom."

I rest my head on his chest. "Tell me about her. You never talk about her. What does she like? Dislike? How did you guys meet? How did you propose? Anything."

"Paris, it's—"

"I know—it's too hard. You say that every time. We talked about her for maybe ten minutes the other day and that was more than the past fifteen years combined. If she's coming back, I need to know more."

"Your mother always had a smile on her face from the day I met her. She's brilliant, kind, loving, full of life, and always serving others. Nothing ever stood in her way and there was never a dull moment with your mom."

"She sounds amazing. How did you guys meet?"

"We met at Harvard. The USI recruited us both, me as a field agent, and your mother as a researcher. During the recruitment process we fell in love. In the end I took the job and she declined."

"Wait, you worked for the USI?"

My dad nods. "I used to. A long time ago, before any of this started."

"How could you work for an organization that hurts people?"

"At the time we didn't. Our sole mission was to protect."

"Maybe they still do, and you're just overreacting? Besides, I can't stay locked up here forever."

"It's not safe."

"Even so, I need to learn how to live with this 'gift.'"

"Finally!"

"What?" I ask.

"Took you long enough. I've been waiting eleven days for you to say that you believe me."

"I didn't mean to be difficult. I believed you since you told me."

"Why didn't you say so?" he asks.

"Sorry, I thought you knew."

He nods. "Well have you experienced anything out of the ordinary besides the episodes yet?"

"No."

"Good. That's good."

"Why is that good?"

"I only know what your mom told me. I want to help you through this but I can only do that if everything happens exactly the way she said it should."

"Why wouldn't it happen the way she said it should?"

"I don't know," he says. "You and your mom were the first."

Everything flashes white and I lose consciousness. When I come to I'm lying on my bed with my dad towering over me.

"Paris, how are you feeling?" he asks.

"Like I have the worst hangover known to man," I say, clutching my head. When will this nightmare end? "How long was I out this time?"

"About an hour. You should get some rest." He walks out the door and closes it behind him.

After a nap I resume another day of the same exact thing. Breakfast, online school, watch a movie, eat some more food, and go to sleep. Sometimes on a good day I can watch two movies, what a life. I miss dance practice, lacrosse, shopping, being with other humans, and even going to school.

I miss Camden. I want him to kiss me, cuddle me, and sing to me like he does when I'm having a bad day. "Say You Won't Let Go" by James Arthur, it's our song. I want to sing it to him right now because I'm never letting go. I've never had anyone I've wanted to sing for. Until now.

The display on my cable box reads ten P.M. Man, time really does fly. I guess it doesn't help when I'm asleep 85% of the day. I change into my warm sweats, brush my teeth, and climb into bed.

Tomorrow—April 30th—will be a better day. I'll be eighteen.

I shoot up out of bed wide-eyed. Something's banging on my window. It's 10:30 P.M.

I crawl out of bed, making my way toward the window. Em? Camden? No way!

"Hey! What are you guys doing here?" I whisper.

"What do you mean, what are we doing here?" Em asks. "We're rescuing you, of course."

"We thought your dad moved you out of the country," Camden says with a smile.

"You guys are the best!" I say. "I have mono but I don't think I'm contagious any longer."

"Well, what are you waiting for? Jump!" Camden says, reaching out his arms.

"Are you crazy?" I ask.

"Would you rather stay locked up in there on your birthday eve," Em asks.

Em and I are starting a tradition that the night before every birthday we take each other out and do something crazy at exactly midnight. This will be the second year and I'm not about to break the tradition, especially on the big eighteen.

"Okay, here I go," I say, climbing through the window. Camden walks to the base of the window, ready to catch me. At least I decided to wear my sweats to bed instead of my nightgown. Okay, don't think, just jump. One, two, three. A cold breeze lines my spine as I fall into love.

Laughter surrounds me. "Par, you can open your eyes now," Camden says.

I open my eyes and look up at him. He caught me. I knew he would. I reach up and place my arms around his neck. He releases my legs and wraps his arms around me. It feels amazing to hug him again. I lean in for one of our short perfect kisses. His soft lips make my entire body tingle.

"Okay, lovebirds," Em says. "Let's get out of here."

"Okay, okay, we're coming," I say. It feels so good to be back with the two of them. "So where are we going?"

"Wouldn't you like to know," Em says.

"Yes, I would like to know."

"Sorry, it's a surprise," Camden says. "You'll just have to deal with the suspense."

"Ugh, you two suck."

"So you have to put these two things on," Em says. She hands me a fancy dress and Camden a blindfold. I walk behind the car and change into the dress. This is one of my favorite of Em's dresses. It's a classy black dress, tight fitting with a beautiful design that sparkles on it. After I finish getting dressed Camden ties the blindfold around my eyes.

"Fancy clothes, this is going to be fun," I say. "But seriously—a blindfold?"

"Tough luck," Camden whispers in my ear.

I'm a dog on a leash with no choice but to do as I'm told. At least the owners are my two best friends. Camden guides me to the car then buckles me in.

"You know this would be a whole lot easier if you just told me where we're going," I say.

"Where's the fun in that?" Em asks.

Em blasts her music and the three of us sing at the top of our lungs. After four songs the car comes to a stop.

"Okay, we're here," Em says." Are you ready for the best night ever?"

"Am I? Get me out of this thing!" I shout. Camden guides me out of the car then takes my blindfold off. "No way. This is so cool! How did you?"

"I got some friends who have friends that were able to get us on the list!" Em says. She's jumping up and down and practically drooling with excitement.

I've always wanted to come here. It's only the coolest club in the state but it's impossible to get in. Especially if you're under twenty-one. They don't serve alcohol, but they tend to stay away from letting high school students in. Em walks over and talks to the security guard, who looks up her name. After he sees it on the list he motions for us to go inside.

It's exactly how I imagined it to be. The dance floor full, everyone partying their hearts out. None of that high school dance crap where you just jump up and down. There's an amazing DJ, a bar, couches in the corner, and lights illuminating the pathway into the dark space.

"This is amazing!" I shout to Em. "Let's dance." I run out onto the dance floor, both Em and Camden following behind me.

Song after song, the three of us are having the time of our lives. I have sweat dripping everywhere. We have been in the middle the entire time, never a dull second. I could stay here forever. But just like with Cinderella the clock strikes midnight and I need to get back.

"Happy birthday!" Em and Camden shout over the music.

"Thank—ahhhhh" I drop to the dance floor in searing pain. What's going on? Make it stop! Please, someone make it stop! I reach up and search my scalp for an entry wound, thinking that I must have been shot or stabbed in the head.

"Paris! Are you okay?" Em shouts.

I can't answer through the pain. I sit up with my head in my hands, holding back tears. Camden helps me up and carries me back to the car.

As Em guns down the road the pain abruptly stops. "I'm okay," I say.

"What happened?" Em asks.

"I think it was just a really really bad migraine. I've been getting them since I got mono."

Em pulled into my driveway and I hugged her and Camden goodbye, thanking them for the night. Regardless of how it ended tonight was still pretty freaking amazing. I climb in through the window on the first floor and sneak back upstairs to my room. This is the first night I've ever successfully snuck out. I redo my nighttime routine, climb into bed, and the second my head hits the pillow I drift off to sleep.

Eighteen Today—Now I Can Buy Some Dry Ice

"AHHHHH!"

"What? What is it?" my dad asks as he barges into my bedroom.

"Ahhhhh! It hurts so bad! Make it stop! Make it stop!"

"What hurts? What do I need to make stop?"

"My head! It hurts! Please Dad, make it stop!" I yell holding my head in my hands.

"It's okay, it's going to be okay." That's all he can do.

"No, it's not. It's hurts so bad." Now I'm begging. I squeeze open an eye and look at the cable box. It's 2:06 A.M. Today's my eighteenth birthday. The first bolt of pain struck exactly at midnight. And this one's twice as painful. How many more are there going to be?

"Oooowwww!" I shriek, tears now streaming down my cheeks. "I just want this pain to go away!"

"Paris, I need you to calm down before you destroy your room."

What? I open my fingers and glance through them. The lights are flashing and everything is shaking—the door, my books, the picture frames on the walls. Even my clothes are falling off their hangers. But I can't focus on that. I sob, clutching my head and letting out the occasional scream.

"Paris, just focus on my voice and try to block out the pain."

"I can't. I can't. I can't."

"Just please try."

"I can't."

"This is not going to stop until you can learn to focus."

"I can't!" I shout. "It hurts so bad. Please. Please, Dad." I'm rocking back and forth cradling my head. The pain's just getting worse. I hear things crashing to the floor.

"Just focus on my voice," he says.

I hear my dad beginning to cry as I scream in agonizing pain. But he continues to talk in the calmest voice he can muster. It works—I finally focus. I focus on his voice and nothing else. Finally I sit up and check the time. It's 3:11 A.M. I was screaming in agonizing pain for more than an hour. I look at my dad. Neither of us have the energy to say anything.

My room is a disaster. The walls have been shaken bare and every piece of glass is broken except for my window. Not a single item of clothing is still hanging. Even the top hinges of my door broke and it's hanging at a weird angle off the wall.

"Dad, why isn't the window broken?" I ask. I mean, the door is basically on the floor.

"Bulletproof windows," he says. "Just in case the USI decides to pay us a visit."

"Oh," I mumble. "What a fantastic way to start my eighteenth birthday." I lie back down in my bed. "I'm exhausted. Goodnight, Dad."

"Goodnight, sweetheart." He kisses my forehead then turns and heads out the door.

∞   ∞   ∞

"Rick!"

I run up to him and give him a big kiss. We're standing in the center of an abandoned barn east of the tiny town of Cedar Fort. One of our many safe houses. "You look handsome—I love this suit. It makes you look like James Bond."

"I love you so much," Rick says. "How are you? Happy anniversary."

"I'm okay. The USI has come close so many times but I'm still here."

He shakes his head. "I hate the idea of you out there being hunted like an animal."

"Whatever, there's really nothing we can do about it."

"I know, I just wish we could be a family again."

"I want nothing more than that as well," I say, wiping the corners of my eyes. "We don't have much time. How's Paris doing with the transition? Is she ready?"

"Ready...? I'm not sure, but the transition is hard. She's more powerful than we thought."

"Have you told her yet?" I ask.

"No, I don't want to overwhelm her."

"But she has a right to know. It's important that she knows."

"Yes, but that doesn't mean it's the right time," Rick says. "She needs to focus on her training, not on him."

"How are you handling it?" I ask. "You doing okay?"

"Every second of it is torture. I just sit there and watch her with no way of helping her stop the pain. It's bringing back too many bad memories of that night. Too many bad memories of everything that happened after."

"Look, I know it's hard, and I know you want to protect her, but she deserves to know the full truth."

"So we're back on this again. She's not ready to know about Tristen. It would destroy her."

∞   ∞   ∞

"Your favorite breakfast for my favorite birthday girl," my dad says. "Happy birthday, sweetheart."

What's going on? I wipe my eyes and sit up. That was a weird dream. It felt so real.

He hands me a wooden platter. Crepes, raspberries and Nutella again? That's two days in a row; he's spoiling me. "Thanks, Dad, this is exactly what I need right now." I give him a grin.

"I have even better news if you can believe it." He pauses for a dramatic effect. "Guess who's going back to school."

"Seriously? I can go back? I can see my friends?" I climb out of bed and jump for joy. "No way! Finally! Thank you, thank you, thank you!"

"You're welcome. I'll leave you to get ready."

All I want is to be at school already. I enjoy every last little bit of my delicious chocolate crepes then grab my phone out of the charger on my desk. Dad restored my service! I plug my phone into my speaker, turn on my music, and get into the shower while belting out the songs in Taylor Swift's new album, Reputation. After a short ten-minute shower, which included my jam session for the day and some of my awesome dance moves, I hop out and grab a towel.

What to wear? I could wear my super cute black dress from American Eagle, or there's always my favorite jean skirt and the cute white t-shirt that I wore on the first day of school. Why does this decision have to be so hard? I need Em to choose for me. In the end I go with my jean skirt and cream t-shirt with black heels and my favorite purse. In this moment life couldn't be better. I'm rocking that outfit, not to sound conceited. I brush my teeth and do my makeup then head downstairs for school.

"Morning again. I'm ready to go."

"Okay, birthday girl," my dad says. "I have one last birthday surprise for you."

"What is it?"

"Follow me." In the driveway is my dream car, a black pickup truck.

"No way! Thank you, thank you, thank you!" I shout, running toward the car. Before I get to it I turn back and run to my dad. "You're the best dad on the planet...thank you." I wrap my arms around him.

"You're welcome. Now go check it out."

I climb into the driver's seat. It's absolutely perfect. "Can I drive to school? Please," I ask, fluttering my eyes.

"I wanted to drop you off so I could make sure you get there safe, but if you promise to—"

"Thank you, thank you, thank you, Daddy! I love you sooo much!"

"You're welcome. But you have to be safe."

"Of course, I promise!" I say. "I better go so I'm not late. Love you!" I shift gears and roll out of the driveway.

"Hey Siri, call Em," I say to my phone.

"Calling Emily Chase."

"Em, I'm on my way to your house to get you."

"Wow!" she exclaims. "You've been freed! Happy birthday!"

"Thanks. Love you, bye," I say hanging up the phone.

I've gained the freedom that comes from being able to drive wherever, whenever, and I already know that I'm going to love it. I roll down all the windows and bask in the glory that is my life.

I turn the corner and see Em waiting for me in her front yard. I pull into her driveway and put the car in park. We both scream as I dive out of the car and break into a run to hug her. I missed her so much. Even though we saw each other last night, it still feels like we haven't been around each other in forever.

"Happy birthday! I love you so much!" Em says.

"I love you more. This has been the longest two weeks of my life!"

"What happened? I want to hear all of the details now that we have time to talk."

Em and I hop into the truck where I make up a story about my mono, how my throat was too sore and swollen to talk and I was sleeping twenty hours a day. Then I ask about school and she gives me the load on all the drama that's been going on so I would be completely caught up. We arrive at the school parking lot, park and just sit, continuing to talk. Five minutes before the bell rings we get out of the truck and head inside.

"Do I look okay?" I turn and ask Em. I can't seem to stop rubbing my sweaty palms against my side.

"Yes, you look beautiful!" Em says. "I love your skirt and your heels."

I didn't realize how difficult it would be to come back. It has been so long and I missed out on so much. I walk through the front door and see Camden. Has he been waiting here for me? He picks me up in a hug then kisses me ever so perfectly. Ugh, I missed this every day. I missed his beautiful face, gorgeous eyes, silky hair, ripped body, dewy lips—I missed everything. Last night was not enough.

"Happy birthday! How are you feeling?" Camden asks, looking straight into my eyes.

"Thanks, and I'm doing great. I feel 110% better." It's true—for some reason I feel amazing. "As much as I want to stay here and kiss you all day, we have to get to class." I lean in to kiss Camden one last time and the three of us head in the direction of our first-period class, AP Physics C, a calculus-based study of Newtonian mechanics and electromagnetism. That's right, my boyfriends hot and a genius. I did good.

We walk into the class and put our stuff down on the table in the back row. The teacher begins a new unit on torque and rotational mechanics. I forgot how exhausting school can be. By the end of his lecture I've taken nine pages of notes. That's insane. The bell rings, signifying we have five minutes to get to our next class. English. I love reading and writing but I don't like English class. I would much rather just have an hour and half set aside to write. But I go anyways.

Next is my favorite class in the world, teachers assistant for Child Development. All we do is take care of kids, feed them, entertain them, and walk them. Not going to lie, I think this class might just be the most beneficial class at this school. Simply because it's the most applicable to life outside of high school. With the things I've learned here I could be an awesome mother.

The bell rings again, this time for lunch. I take back what I said earlier—lunch is actually the best part of the day. I meet Em and Camden in the parking lot and drive them to Marco's for lunch. Pizza: the only food group needed for survival.

"So, how's your day been so far?" Camden asks, at least I think. It's hard to tell what he's saying while shoving pizza down his throat.

"It's been great," I say trying and failing to keep a straight face. I break out in laughter. Em and Camden join in and our lunch turns into a laughing fit.

We return to school and head to our AP Calculus class. At least we have it together. Our teacher, Mr. Nelson, is the best teacher in the school. If you need help he will stay till midnight if he has to until it makes sense. Sometimes he even lets students come over on a Saturday to get help with the homework if they need it. I've never met a nicer man.

As the class progresses he begins to go into more depth about antiderivatives and integrals. Again I take pages of notes while following along. After the bell rings for the final time of the day Em and Camden head toward the commons while I stay behind to take a test I missed in Calc.

An hour and a half of pure misery passes. I'm not a fan of calc tests—they're incredibly hard—but I'm pretty sure I just aced it. Now all I want is to go home and hang out with Camden and Em. It is nice to be back, but I forgot how much I don't like sitting in almost two-hour-long classes. I leave the room and start for the commons. On a normal day they would have just gone home but seeing as it's my first day back they wanted to be here when I finished. Plus I'm Em's ride.

I walk down the long tile hallways lined by maroon lockers. I don't see a single other person in the halls but me. Where is everyone? There are always tons of kids and at least a few teachers. I search the commons but there's no sign of Em and Camden anywhere. I continue my search around the rest of the school. I walk all the way to the end of the school by the 800 hall. The last place to check.

I hear voices around the corner. They don't sound like students—maybe teachers? I can't make out what they're saying.

"Where ... no ... call ... find ... now ..." I wonder if it's private? Whatever, I have to find Camden and Em. I run my hand along the wall as I turn the corner toward the direction of the voices.

At the end of 800 hall there is a tiny passageway that connects to the 700 hall. I peek around the corner. Why are there guys in suits here? None of the teachers dress like that. They're surrounding Camden and Em. The USI? No. No. This can't be happening. I have to text my dad.

How do they know about me? Calm down, Paris, maybe you're wrong.

I make eye contact with Em and she mouths the word "run."

I can't just leave my friends. But maybe if I'm not here the USI will leave them alone. I quietly start to back away. Then, of course, I bump into a locker with a metallic clang. All eyes turn toward me.

"Oh hey, Hannah. How's it going?" Em says.

"That's her," says one of the men.

"Nooooo!" Em shouts.

"Don't take another step, or it will be the last step you take," I say in a pathetic attempt to scare them. Hopefully they know somewhat of what I'm capable of, because I have no idea.

All seven men freeze. I try to cover up my look of bewilderment with something more intimidating although I'm not sure it's working.

"Paris, my name is Crew," says the agent closest to me. "We don't want to hurt you. But we are under direct orders to bring you in, one way or another."

"Whatever you have is no match for me," I say.

Crew smiles. "We know that today is your first day with the Gift. You have no idea how to use it."

I smile back. "Wanna test that theory?" I squint my eyes and focus so hard on the men that I feel lightheaded. How do they know that today is the first day? Only my dad knows that.

The agents exchange a look. "I'm sorry it's come to this but we'll have to take your friends if you don't come," Crew says. He gestures toward his men and four of them grab Em and Camden.

"They have nothing to do with this," I say.

"It's okay, Par. We'll go with them as long as you get out of here," Em says. She would sacrifice herself for me without even knowing why. I wish I had told them.

"Run!" Camden shouts, leaping on one of the agents. Two of the others join the pile as another drags Em outside. A tear runs down my face. My world is falling apart, and I may never see them again.

I turn and run.

The men chase after me. I sprint as fast as I can to the 700 hall, then the 600.

"Paris, we have your dad too," Crew shouts after me. "You need to cooperate."

I freeze. My dad? No, they can't have my dad. I turn around.

"We picked him up this morning," Crew says, slowing to a walk. "How else do you think we could have known it was your birthday? Or that you were exposed this morning? Hurt, didn't it?"

I lower my head. It's true. My dad always texts me in between classes. He's so overprotective. Crew and the other two agents grab my arms and drag me toward the door.

No. I'm not letting this happen. If they have my dad they're not getting me too. He would want me to fight. And he needs me to rescue him. I scream on the top of my lungs and push the men off me. They go flying in all directions, smashing into lockers and falling unconscious to the floor. Whoa. What?

No time to think. I have to save Em and Camden and get as far away from here as possible.

I sprint back toward the 800 hall, then out the back door into the overflow parking lot. Em and Camden are tied up in the back seat of a black sedan. I duck behind the trashcan beside the doorway and peer around it. Two men sit in the front seats of the car and one stands outside the car. Em and Camden are banging on the windows, shouting on the top of their lungs, trying to get the attention of anyone they can, but there's no one else here. The agent keeping guard pulls his gun and angrily raps the butt against the window. I don't know what to do. I envision smacking their heads together and knocking them unconscious, but nothing happens. I close my eyes, focusing on the men. Maybe if I concentrate hard enough something will happen like the last time.

∞ ∞ ∞

When I open my eyes again someone who looks like my mom is standing in front me. We're standing on a beach in the middle of a brilliantly sunny day. Shimmering turquoise water stretches out to the horizon.

"Sophie, you have to focus," my mom says to me. Am I in someone else's body? I take a step to the side and see a second girl behind where I was standing. She's a cute blond, similar to me. Lots of freckles.

"Mom, it's me, Paris." No response. "Hello? Mom? Nikki?" Again nothing. This is exactly like the dream before. I walk up to touch my mom, and my hand goes right through her. Yep, the exact same thing.

Panic rises up in me. I have to save Em and Camden. I have to get back.

I try everything to wake up. Pinching, slapping, and now I'm to my last resort—waiting. I sit down on the warm sand and watch my mom and Sophie.

"I can't do this! I give up!" Sophie shouts and storms away. Suddenly she can't move. She levitates in the air and floats back to where she was previously standing. She's stiff as a board—I can't even tell if she's breathing. Then she drops back onto the beach.

"If you want to be able to do what I just did, it's going to take a lot of practice," my mom says. "Understand?"

"Yes," Sophie groans.

My mom moved Sophie so effortlessly. No flinch, no eye squinting. I can't imagine what that would feel like—good, bad?

"The best way is to clear your brain entirely," my mom says in a quiet calming voice. "Nothing but empty space. Good. Now think about lifting just a few grains of sand.

You have to start small. Picture it in your mind, picture the grains lifting into the air. Close your eyes if it helps."

Sophie focuses on my mother's words as if her life depends on it. She closes her eyes and grains begin to rise. Not many, but a handful of sand lifts off the ground.

"Now don't lose your focus," my mother says. "It's important that you continue to think about what you're doing." My mother pauses as more sand beings to rise. "Open your eyes, but remember to remain focused. Don't get too excited and drop them." Sophie opens her eyes and a giant grin widens her face. She did it. Now there's a hundred handfuls' worth of sand floating in the air.

∞　　∞　　∞

I blink and there's no more warm brilliant beach, no more shimmering blue water. Now it's my turn to try to lift the sand. It's my time to try to save my friends.

Listen

HOW MUCH TIME HAVE I LOST? None, apparently. Em and Camden are still locked in the car and held at gunpoint.

I remember my mother's calming words. Clear your brain entirely. Nothing but empty space. You have to start small and work big. Picture it in your mind. Don't lose your focus.

A brief gust of wind pushes an empty soda can across the parking lot. I'll start with that. I close my eyes and clear my brain. I picture it lifting up and hovering in the air. I open my eyes only thinking of the can. And nothing. I repeat the process with the same result. Why can't I do this? Am I not good enough?

No! I can do this!

I don't close my eyes this time. I stare into the can and demand that it rise. With no question it lifts off the ground. I try moving it side to side, and it follows. Now up and down, it follows. It's not a matter of deep focus to make the objects move. I have to believe in myself. I have to want it to move and believe that it can. And now it's time to rescue Em and Camden.

First I have to take care of the guard on the outside. Small, then big. I already did small, that pathetic soda can. Now big, his body. I imagine myself inside of his body and try to make him move. Nothing. But I know I can do this. I take a different approach. I picture the USI agent as the can. A giant can. I lift the agent and throw him against a tree. He falls to the ground unconscious. 'Yesss' I scream inside.

My attention turns back to the car. From behind the trashcan, I use my new gift to open the back car door. Then I make the two guards in the front seats slam their heads together. They both fall forward, lying motionless against the dash. As I run toward the car, I hear a gunshot and feel a white-hot flash pain in my left shoulder. I drop to my knees. Camden and Em are running towards me. Two more shots ring out and they drop to the ground.

All three of us get off the ground and run. We just need to make it around the corner of the school.

More gunshots. A bullet snaps through the air just inches from my head. Then we're around the corner—safe, for at least a second.

"Where is he? Where are the shots coming from?" I ask bending over and breathing deeply, trying to push the pain out of my mind.

"Paris, thank goodness," Em says, hugging me. I grunt with the effort of stifling a scream.

Em quickly lets go and takes a step back.

"Oh my gosh, Paris, you're bleeding," Camden says.

"We can worry about that later," I say. "Right now we have to get out of this alive." They follow me as I head toward the side door to the school. We need to get to my truck in the front parking lot.

We slip through the side door and creep down the hallway. We pass the three USI agents that I'd taken out earlier. They're still unconscious (or worse?), but we still have the gunman to deal with.

When we get to the front doors, Camden ducks into a crouch and inches to one of the windows. "I don't see anybody," he says as he peers out. "Come on."

We file out, constantly checking behind us and to our left and right. "Where could he be?" I mumble to myself.

More gunshots. We duck, not knowing where to turn.

"Paris, he's to your left!" Em shouts. I see him. He stands across the parking lot, pointing his gun at me. But not for long. He flings it away as I take control of his arm. Then I pick him up and throw him to the ground. He lies motionless. This time I hope he's dead.

"How...how did that just happen?" Em asks, taking two steps back from me.

Guess the secret's out. "It's a long story. I promise I'll tell it later, but can we please get out of here first?"

Em takes two more steps back. "How?" she asks again, shaking her head. "It's not possible."

"I know. Please, Em. It's still me. Please, let's just get out of here." I take her hand and we rush to my truck. Blood is streaming down my left arm as I climb into the passenger seat. I need to get the bullet out.

Why isn't Camden saying anything? He doesn't even look surprised. Why hasn't he tried to hold me? I don't understand.

What do we do now? They have my dad. My mom's MIA. I don't know who to trust. Where do we go? Who do we see for my shoulder? Can we trust the hospital?

But next—I don't know what from, maybe the loss of blood, the stress, or something Gift related, but next—blackness.

∞   ∞   ∞

I wake up and see a bright light shining down on me. There's a steady beeping sound to my left. Crap, this is a hospital.

"Em? Camden?"

"We're right here," Em says. "Don't worry. We're right here with you and we're never going to leave you." She climbs onto my bed and runs her hand down my hairline. Camden says nothing. Maybe he's in shock.

"What happened?" I ask Em since she seems to be the only person functioning.

"You passed out. I told the doctors that you were out hunting and you tripped and shot yourself. I know it's not a great story, but it was hard to come up with something on the spot."

"No, thank you, that was the perfect lie."

"Oh, and I gave them a fake name in case someone here worked with the USI."

"Thank you. You're the best." I glance over at Camden who is still sitting in the chair in the corner, not saying a single word. "How long have I been out?"

"Hours," Em says. "The nurse hooked you up to an IV. She said she was giving you some pain meds and something to help you sleep since that was the best way to recover."

"Okay, thank you."

"Par."

"Yes?"

"I think it's time for you to explain what happened," Em says in a firm voice. "Is this why you were out of school for so long?"

"Okay, let me start from the very beginning…"

I tell them the very long story starting at the lab, sparing no details.

"Now that you know the full story, please don't freak out," I say. "And please believe me. Do you believe me?"

Silence still from Camden. He's making me nervous. What if he doesn't keep my secret? What if he thinks I'm some kind of freak?

"Do you?" I ask again.

"I want to say that you're crazy," Em begins, "that everything you just said is impossible, ridiculous. But I can't. I believe you. Of course I believe you. I saw you. I saw everything you did."

"Thank you Em!" I reach to hug her—ouch, my arm. With all this brainpower you would think I could make myself heal. Well, who knows how much I can really do—maybe I'll learn how.

I look over at Camden who still stares into nothingness. "Camden? What are you thinking?" I ask.

"I…I believe you, of course," he says. "I'm just…I don't know what to think." He turns and looks away, hunching over in his seat.

"Par, there's something I should probably tell you," Em says. "At the time I thought it was all a coincidence, and that we had awful timing, but now I know better…"

"What?"

Em purses her lips. "Remember when you passed out in my bathroom and then woke up in your bed?"

"Yeah, of course."

"Well we didn't tell you the whole story."

"She doesn't need to hear this right now," Camden says. "Let her rest."

"No, it's important that she knows everything," Em says. "It might be important to her."

Camden frowns and shakes his head but doesn't protest further.

"It all started after you passed out in the bathroom," Em says. "When you fell and Camden came running in, it looked like you were having some sort of seizure. When we tried to call your dad, none of our phones would work. Then the lights started flickering. It was like that with anything electrical around you. It was like you were an EMP. We managed to get you home but as we did, light posts shut off as we drove by them, then turned back on when we were a couple feet past them. And you didn't stop shaking the entire time either. When we got to your house we gave you to your dad and told him the story. And then I forgot all about it until I saw you move that guy. Almost like a mental block, and I don't know what caused it."

"Camden, did you forget too?" I ask.

"Yeah, it seemed like it all came back to me around the same time as Em."

"That's weird. Do you think I could have caused your memory loss?" I ask, then instantly regret the question.

"You may have without knowing," Em says, "or maybe something else could have caused it. It seems like anything's possible now."

"True." I don't think it was me or the USI ... Could my dad have erased their memories? I mean, he didn't want Em and Camden to know anything about this. Maybe he used some fancy gadget to block their memory. Or maybe he didn't.

I'm too tired for this, and my arm hurts too much. "I think I'm going to take a nap," I say. "And as soon as I wake up, it's probably going to be time for us to hit the road—if you still want to come with me, that is. I need to find my mom. She has the answers and will know how to rescue my dad." I look at both Em and Camden, "You don't have to answer now. Think about it and let me know when I wake up."

Em and Camden look at each other, both most likely unsure of what they'll do. As for me, I close my eyes in hopes that I can fall asleep.

∞   ∞   ∞

My alarm goes off and I jump out of bed. It's time to go to school. I look out the window and stop. This isn't Alpine. Where am I? I shouldn't be at home anyway—I was just in the hospital and now I'm in some stranger's bedroom in the middle of a forest? I have to find my mom. I have to save my dad.

When I hear a knock on my door I hurry to the closet and lock myself inside. A woman walks in, wearing a pink dress. Mom? I walk out of the closet knowing she would never hurt me.

"Morning, Bella," she says. "Breakfast is ready."

What? Bella? I try to touch my mom and of course my hand goes right through her. Another dream. If I can even call it that.

I look back and see another girl standing by the closet. She must be about eighteen years old. She has brown hair and is super tiny. How is it that my mom can be a mother to all these girls? And love them when she doesn't love me! I should be her first priority but I'm not a priority at all.

My mom begins to lecture Bella about some Gift-related topic that I find very unimportant. So instead of listening, I begin to walk around and try to find out where they are— maybe they'll still be there. That's somewhere to start at least, since I have no leads whatsoever.

I walk through the bedroom doorway directly into the kitchen. There's a bed on the floor, probably where my mom sleeps. I wonder how long they've been hiding out in this tiny wooden shed in the middle of nowhere. How deep is the USI into everything if they have to hide this drastically? I need to get back. I need to get out of this hospital. Even with a fake name, it's not safe. It wasn't safe the first time I was in the hospital and I'm not safe now. And what if it wasn't an accident that put me into the hospital the first time? What if a USI agent was the one who tried to kill me?

The last time I was admitted to the hospital, I nearly died. I was eleven years old and had gone hiking with my dad. Let's just say that was not the best day ever. It was my first time hiking and I'm kinda accident prone. And well, I kinda slipped a little and everything's a blur from there. The next thing I remember is doctors everywhere, blood everywhere, tons of needles and drugs. Lots of life support—you know, the usual when you fall down a cliff.

My dad tells me that I was very lucky—not only once, but twice. See, once I got to the hospital I almost died again. For some reason my life support failed. A nurse rushed in—who I've always remembered as my mother since they looked so similar—and she saved me, obviously, or I wouldn't be here now. But it was close. Too close for me to ever trust a hospital again.

I need to get out of this dream, back to reality, and out of the hospital. I try pinching and slapping myself again, and of course it doesn't work. I guess I have to wait until I learn whatever message this dream is trying to convey.

I look around and try to figure out where I could possibly be. I head outside and no luck. All there is are woods. I feel bad for Bella, getting dragged away from everything she must know and love to live with my mom in a shack in the middle of the forest.

I head back inside and into the only bedroom. No decorations on the walls, just a plain old crappy kid's-sized bed.

"Now that you know the plan, we can begin training for the day," my mom says.

Crap! I missed the plan.

"Okay, just to make sure I understand correctly—"

Or maybe I will!

"—we're going to leave Pole Hill in about a week and head to…where?" Bella asks.

"Your training will be complete, so you will return home. And leave this part of your life a secret. But you will remain alert because at a moment's notice, your life may change drastically."

First stop, Pole Hill. I'll have to google it when I wake up.

"Okay, I'm ready," Bella says with her game face on. I follow them back outside.

"Today you will learn how to read another's mind," my mom says. "This is a very important part of the Gift. It allows you to know who you can trust, and eventually you will be able to control the thoughts of others."

Cool! Like mind control.

"The first step to reading someone's mind is not to clear your own. This time you must focus all your attention to your ears. It's almost as if you're trying to hear the thoughts of others. It will open up a connection that you can use to either hear their thoughts or allow them to hear your thoughts. They will always go along with your demands or opinions. For example, if I read your mind and heard you think that this is stupid, I could use the connection and say that this is in fact very cool. The next time I read your mind, you would think that this is very cool."

My mom takes a few steps back. "But let's not get ahead of ourselves. First we start with simply trying to hear my thoughts."

Bella closes her eyes.

"Bella, there's no need to close your eyes. The only thing that matters are your ears. Start by really listening to the sounds that surround you."

I do the same and find that I can hear frogs croaking, crickets chirping, birds singing, and so many more sounds.

"Now turn your attention to me and focus on the things outside of my head, like the sound of my voice or the sounds of my fleece vest cracking in the wind."

I sit and try to pick out the individual sounds that surround my mom.

"Good. Now turn your attention to my head, listen to my thoughts."

I try to focus but I can't seem to hear anything. Maybe it won't work in the dream. I close my eyes, trying to focus on the sounds. Still nothing.

$$\infty \qquad \infty \qquad \infty$$

When I open my eyes, she's gone. No more forest or croaking frogs. I'm back in the hospital with my friends. Desperate to know the next move.

"Paris? ... Paris?" Em asks.

I tune out her voice and listen to the sound of her rapid breathing, and the tinkle of her bracelet as she waves her arms in front of my eyes. Then I listen to her hair as it sways in the air, and the sound of her eyes opening and closing as she blinks. Now it's time for her thoughts.

Paris! We need to get out of here. Why won't you wake up? I don't know what to do.

Oh, Em, I respond, please don't be scared. I'll keep you safe. I listen to her thoughts again but they haven't changed. That's something that I will need to master another day.

"Par?" Em whispers.

"Yes, sorry," I say. "I'm here."

"I think we need to leave. I have a feeling that it's not safe here anymore."

"I know."

"How do you know? You've slept the whole time."

"I just mean I know that we've been in one place for too long." I don't think they're ready to know that their thoughts are no longer safe as well. That's a whole 'nother level of invasion of privacy.

"How long was I out?" I ask.

"About three hours," Camden says. He looks sad. "So what's the plan?" Camden asks with dreary eyes.

"Well that depends. What have you guys decided to do?"

"I'm going to come with you, help you find your mom and dad, and stop the USI," Em says. Her face is strained and she doesn't look certain at all.

Camden sighs. "I'm going to come with you as well. You're my girlfriend—I'm not going to let you face this on your own. Plus we always wanted to go on a road trip together."

I want to read his mind and find out what he really thinks. But I can't invade his privacy like that. He would be so mad if he ever found out. Besides, it doesn't matter—he's coming, and Em's coming.

I smile. "Well, then it's settled. Pole Hill, here we come!"

"Where's that?" Camden asks.

My smile falters. "I'm not sure. It's a forest, or in one."

"So why would we go there?" he asks.

"I'll explain on the way."

Em whips out her phone and starts thumbing away. "There's a Pole Hill in Utah. Fishlake National Forest, three hours south of here. Looks like there's lots of trees around."

I jump out of bed. "Let's do it!"

CHAPTER 6

Pole Hill

THE THREE OF US slide out of the car and stare in amazement at the grand view below us. We're parked at the summit of Joseph Peak. Green stretches on forever. All that's left is to drive down and begin the search.

"We made it!" I exclaim.

"I wouldn't be so sure about that," Camden says.

"What's that supposed to mean?" Em asks.

"How on earth are we supposed to find a little small cabin in all of this? We'd be better off finding a needle in a haystack."

"Are we in third grade now?" Em said. "A needle in a haystack, really?"

"Cut the sarcasm."

Em punches his arm. "I'll stop being sarcastic when you stop being pessimistic. Like that will ever happen."

Camden smiles for the first time. "Now who's the pessimist?"

"I wasn't being pessimistic—I was being snarky."

"That's one word for—"

"Okay, okay, I interrupt. "Let's get going. The sooner we get down there the sooner we can get some answers."

The three of us hop back into the car and begin the twenty-minute drive through the forest surrounding Pole Hill. Em is back on her phone, wincing as she scrolls.

"Your parents?" I ask.

"Par, they're never going to forgive me. They're so mad. I told them that I decided to go to the audition in New York. I said I never told them because I knew they would say no."

"Em, I'm so sorry, I know you really did want to go to that audition."

"It's okay. There'll always be more. And I wasn't lying when I said I knew they wouldn't let me go. I told them I'd come home as soon as the audition is over, and that calmed them down a little."

"But that's only a few days. We might be gone for... well, a long time, maybe even months..." I say.

"I'll just keep calling every week then and extend the trip," Em says. "First callbacks, then a final audition, then I got the part, and finally practices. Plus my family's leaving for Europe on that big trip soon so they'll be distracted."

"Em, you're a genius."

"I know," she says while flipping her hair.

"Camden, what did your parents say?" I ask.

"You mean foster parents," he snaps.

Camden doesn't like to talk about his home life. He mentioned once that his parents were in some accident when he was younger and he and his little brother have been bouncing from foster family to foster family ever since. One time I convinced Camden to take me to dinner with his foster parents; they seemed nice.

"I told them I was taking some time to travel and figure out what I want to do with my life," he adds. "There isn't anything they can do. I'm eighteen and legally out of the system."

Camden stops the car a few minutes later. "Okay this is it," he says, turning off the ignition. "We'll have to walk from here."

"That was fast, nice driving," I say, leaning in for a kiss. He turns away and gets out of the car. "What's wrong, Camden?"

"Let's get walking," he says. "It's going to take weeks to find this cabin."

"Shouldn't we pull the car into the woods?" Em asks. "If somebody sees it on the road that could lead the USI to us."

Camden sighs and tosses her the keys. "Be my guest."

We search for hours with no luck. The sun has begun to set and in a couple of minutes it's going to be pitch black. The three of us begin to set up camp. Em and I set up the tent while Camden goes off looking for firewood.

My dad was very prepared and had stashed three backpacks behind the front bench seat of my new truck. In the woods hospital parking lot I grabbed the backpacks and, well, stole a car, I guess. Another trick that my dad had taught me when we were on the road. I felt bad about it, but we couldn't risk driving my truck.

The backpacks were tightly packed with everything you'd need if society collapsed—a tent, some blankets, a medical kit with antibiotics and multivitamins, a flashlight and plenty of cash, solar chargers, batteries, and a whole backpack filled with nonperishable food—dried fruit, vegetables, and salmon, and a whole bunch of energy bars. And most important for us, money—about $15,000 cash. The backpacks were equipped with water purifiers but we'd stopped at a gas station to supplement that with a couple of gallons of bottled water.

After setting up camp we're exhausted, and sleep comes almost immediately.

Day after day continues in the same pattern. Walking around in the woods, finding nothing, getting exhausted and cranky, then bed. I think all of us could use new scenery right about now—and I'm not just talking about this forest. We ran out of things to talk about around day two. We've walked so many miles that I'm sure I've lost at least five pounds by now.

On the plus side, I've been able to practice with the Gift for hours. Every once and awhile I would stop and try to pick up some rocks, starting at the smallest and working to the heaviest I could find. Then I practiced knocking a tree over. It took some strength but eventually it went down. I think I'm getting the hang of it. And I'm getting a little better at reading Em's mind. It doesn't take as long as it did the first time. But I still can't seem to convince her that Ed Sheeran is the hottest guy in the universe. Maybe I should try something more believable, like that bell-bottoms are back in style. I wish my mom were here to train me.

"Okay, I think it's about time we give up on this cabin," I say as we pack up our camp the next morning. "I guess the dreams are just dreams. Either that or my mom's just too good of a hider."

"Are you sure?" Camden asks. "You were pretty set on this idea."

"So where are we going next?" Em asks.

The two of them stare at me like puppies at the pound. I don't want to make all the decisions. But I'm the one with the Gift, and I'm just going to have to accept that.

"We'll just have to find a new lead and go off of that," I say. "Let's get back to the car."

We've been searching in a spiral pattern, making a large circle and gradually working our way in. So even though it took us three days to get to this point, it will only take about a half a day to cut straight through the center and get back to our stolen car.

"Seriously, Par, where are we going to go?" Em asks.

"I'm not sure," I say. "Any place you particularly wanted to see?"

"I'm being serious, Paris. What's the plan? Because we can't just go wherever hoping to find your mom. And what happens once we run out of money, or what if the USI finds us, and take us?" Em's voice accelerates as her panic rises. I grab her arm.

"Em, calm down. I want to tell you that everything is going to work out, but I don't know what I'm doing anymore than you do. I don't know what you want me to say." I let go of her arm and try to smile. "But if something occurs to you, please let me know."

"Paris!" Camden shouts from up ahead. "Paris, help!"

I take off running toward the road up ahead. The USI, they're here. They found us. And here I was thinking that maybe I could do this, but they found us with no trouble at all.

Four new cars are parked in a semicircle around ours. There are more than a dozen agents—two of them restraining Camden and the rest training their guns on me. I don't recognize any of them from the attack at my school.

"Stand down, Paris. You know that we're not going to stop until you come with us."

"This isn't going to go down any better for you than the last time," I shout. I throw a fist and the man standing next to their apparent leader goes flying up the slope and across the road. A telekinesis super punch? Who knew.

"Don't shoot her," the first man says. "We need her alive." He looks back at me. "But try that again and we'll shoot your friend." The men switch their target from me to Em. "Come with us and we won't hurt her."

I ignore him and focus my attention on their guns. Their hands jerk to the side but they don't let go. Okay, time for plan B. Before they can aim back at Em I press in the button on the mag and all of their clips fall to the ground. Then I twist down their arms and pull the triggers so that their guns fire at the ground.

"Em, hide," I say.

Anger begins to show through on their faces. All of the men but the two who are holding Camden charge at me. I take two deep breaths then let the Gift take over. I punch one on my right, knocking him unconscious, then turn to my left and fling two agents back into the trees. Jab, duck, jab, jab, duck, two more are down. An agent grabs me from behind and pins me to the ground. I roll back and forth but he's too strong to shake.

"Get the cuffs," he shouts.

Cuffs? No, not today.

I swing up a leg, catching him in the crouch. He rolls off and I slide him across the ground into a tree. I jump up and lift two men charging at me high into the sky. They fall back through the branches of canopy with a shatter like breaking glass. I'm grabbed from behind again but I'm ready this time, dropping him with an elbow that shatters his nose. Now I'm facing only two of them, and it's easy work to dispatch them both. I crack my knuckles, but I'm pretty sure I don't look as cool as I feel.

"Valiant effort," the leader calls out.

"When will you just give up?" I ask.

He nods over his shoulder as two men drag an unconscious Em out of the woods. One of them is holding a gun to her head.

"Looks like you're going to have to choose," he says, turning back to the road. One of the two agents restraining Camden is holding a gun to his head as well.

"You wouldn't," I shout.

"Try me."

I want to charge at him. Kill him. But I can't, I need to think. I can't release the clips or they could kill my friends before I take care of the bullets in the chamber. I guess I'm just going to have to be fast. I throw the two agents off Em then whip around to save Camden. The lead agent swings his gun around at Camden and fires at the same time as I throw the two agents into the trees across the road. Camden cries out in pain and drops to the ground.

The last remaining agent, the leader, walks over and stands directly over Camden. He cocks his gun and grins at me. When I recover from my shock I slide Camden out from under him and down to me.

"Are you okay?" I ask.

"I don't know," he says. Blood is spreading across the wound on his thigh.

Before I can help him, my eyes scan for the final agent—he's walking away. Is he giving up? Whatever he's not a threat right now, so Camden is the priority.

I search the back of his jeans for the exit wound. There isn't one, so the bullet must have gotten lodged in the bone. I use telekinesis to carefully pull it out. Then I unbutton Camden's shirt and tie it tightly over the wound. I glance up—the final agent is rummaging through the back seat of his car. Em has woken up and is sitting groggily in the dirt.

"Can you walk?" I ask. We hobble over to Em with his arm around my neck. She stands up and takes him from me.

"Em, how are you?" I ask.

"I'm fine. Let's just go. Watch out for more agents."

The three of us are halfway up the slope when the final agent calls out from behind us. He just won't quit.

He throws another pair of handcuffs at Camden, who reaches out and catches them with his free hand. Em lets go of him and I catch him before he can fall.

"Are you serious?" I shout. "We're not surrendering. We've won!"

"But Terrence…" Camden says.

"Do it!" the man shouts.

I hear a click as Camden locks a handcuff around my left wrist and I instinctively leap away.

"Camden?" I ask. "What's going on? How do you know his name?"

"I'm sorry. I don't have a choice."

I stare at him directly in the eyes, confused, scared, hurt, pissed. Then I drop him to the ground with a single punch and charge at the final agent, Terrence. Rage fills my soul with every step. Somehow he managed to turn Camden. He lunges for his car, and I pull him back. I grab him by the hair and slam his head into my knee. He drops to his knees and I slam the side of his head into his car.

Em and I quickly gather the backpacks and load them into the back seat. We're in too much shock to speak as we drive away. Em just keeps driving south. I mess around with the cuff until I finally smash it open. Instantly I feel a burst of energy, almost as if the cuffs were inhibiting the Gift. After my adrenaline rush fades the pain from the bullet wound in my shoulder is overwhelming. But I can't focus on anything other than Camden. Camden's with the USI? I can't seem to wrap my head around it. Was our relationship just one big lie from the start? Was he working for them the entire time?

"Paris, what do we do?" Em asks with tears streaming down her cheeks.

"I—" Come on, Paris, pull yourself together— "we need to ditch this car. They'll be looking for it. After that we'll head to a train station."

"And go where?"

"Wherever the train takes us." It may not be the best thing to do, but it's something. The USI is everywhere. But even if running away from some agents is just running towards others, we need to feel safe for a moment. At least we would have a moment to rest on the train. If I'm going to black out again, I need to be somewhere I know I can't be hurt.

We pass through a small town and get directions to their closest train station, which is apparently in Helper, Utah. Em parked the car a couple of blocks away (with a sweet note and a small thank you for their trouble, expressed as $300) then we walked to a little one-building train station. We have two choices—east toward Chicago or west toward California. I check the timetables then buy us two tickets to Winnemucca, Nevada. That'll give me more than enough time to rest and recover and since we'll be arriving there in the middle of the night, I can steal another car while everyone's asleep.

When the train rolls in an hour later Em and I settle into our seats in the car all the way in the back. Em had to stow our backpacks because I can barely lift my arms. Using this much energy is causing my body to stop functioning. My mind is still alert, but my body won't respond like I tell it to. Maybe I need to work out more, add some cardio to my daily activities, which so far only consist of me running for my life.

"Camden," I moan. "Camden." I feel hands on my arms shaking me awake.

"Par, wake up."

"Camden." I shoot up awake and reach out for him. He's gone—it wasn't a dream. I'm alone with Em in the dim car as the train rattles through the night.

"Paris, we have to get off soon."

"It wasn't a dream."

"I know," Em says as she wraps her arms around me. Tears flood out, soaking her shirt. "I know." She holds me while I pull myself together. I rip his necklace off and throw it to the floor.

"Paris, I know you're not ready to talk—"

"No, I'm ready. So he's with the USI—what does that mean for us? He was sending them updates? Telling them when the Gift activated, where we would be, what my strengths and weaknesses are? I'm such an idiot."

"No, you couldn't have known," Em says.

"I could have read his mind. I should have read his mind. I was trying to give him privacy, but I'm such an idiot."

"There's nothing we can do about it now so don't beat yourself up over it."

"I loved him. I love him. I let him in and he was faking the entire time. We were so happy, it felt so real. I don't know how to get over him but I know you're right—we need to move on. He's out of my life for good and if I ever see him again, I'll kill him."

"Paris, come on."

"Okay, I won't kill him but everything I once felt for him, all that love, it's gone. It's all gone and there's only pure hatred left." It's time to move on. If I don't then he wins. "Is there anything we told him that could hurt us?"

"Well, he knows about the dreams, but we decided those weren't real. And we don't even know where we're going, so."

"So we're safe. For now."

"Right," Em says. "You ready?"

"Yeah, I'm ready." I stand up and grab a backpack from the overhead shelf as the train pulls into the station. "We'll get a car, then lie low for awhile. The USI's probably already figured out that we took this train, so we can't stay here. I was thinking West Texas. Does that sound good to you?"

"Sounds perfect."

"Great. And then we'll come up with a plan. We're going to put an end to the USI."

Em smiles. "Well then, what are we waiting for?"

∞   ∞   ∞

Night after night Em and I bounce from hotel room to hotel room in West Texas. Waiting for another dream. Anything to go off of. A destination. A person. A new way to use the Gift. Anything. These dreams, they trap me inside, a sick form of torture, and don't let me out until I've learned the lesson. But I can't complain because it's the only training I'm getting.

It's been a week of the same thing, and we're sick of it. Wake up, clean up, find a new hotel, watch crappy television while eating fast food we bought at the drive through. Em buys a burner phone from time to time so she can update her parents on her progress in New York. I don't have anyone to call so I'm still on my first one.

The fire we once had to take action is dwindling and I don't know how much longer we can keep it alive. I've begged for a new dream and I'm starting to lose both hope and my temper. Send me a new dream, Mom. Help me. Where do I go?

Go to Mexico.

What the crap is in Mexico? That's a stupid idea. Come on, Paris, think.

Mexico.

There's nothing in Mexico. Whatever, I'll have a dream eventually.

More days pass of the same routine. Wake up, clean up, find a new hotel, watch crappy television while eating fast food we bought at the drive through. And every day I have the same thought—Mexico. Maybe I'm beginning to lose my mind for real. Anyways, "Mexico" isn't helpful— that's a huge country.

Mexico.

I know, I know, Mexico.

"Em, I know this is going to sound crazy, but I can't shake this thought that we should go to Mexico."

"Okay..." she says. "Why Mexico?"

"I don't know," I admit.

"Where in Mexico?"

"I don't know that either."

"How are we going to get there? We can't cross the border in a stolen car. And we don't have passports."

I laugh. "I don't know! All I know is I have this recurring thought that Mexico is our answer. And it feels like the thought isn't mine."

"Par, that doesn't make any sense."

"I told you it would sound crazy, but what do we have to lose?"

"I guess you're right. Mexico it is. How are we going to get across the border?"

"I have an idea for that. First we need to buy a cheap car and get on the road." Or get someone to drive us—that'll save some cash. I think I might have finally mastered mind control. I've been practicing every day, and most of the time people accept my thoughts. Em's been humming a lot of Ed Sheeran songs lately. The border's not that far, only about a thirty-minute drive.

"Let's go then," Em says while packing up her things. We check out of our hotel and drive to a taco stand that I'll remember fondly for the rest of my life. I kindly ask a young man for a lift to Mexico. He accepts my thought.

As he drives us to the border, I'm staring out the window when everything goes white and a new thought pops into my head. A picture of the world. It zooms in on North America. Now the junction of Mexico, West Texas, and New Mexico. It zooms in further to a little town about a hundred miles south of the border. Villa Ahumada. Then a street name, Ayuntamiento.

"Paris, we're at the border, now what?" Em asks, snapping me back to reality.

When it's our turn at border control, I tell the officer to let us through. He accepts the thought and waves us on. I tell the stranger driving us to take Federal Highway 45 through the city and then south to Villa Ahumada.

Once we arrive, Em and I hop out of the car. I give our driver some cash and tell him to return home.

"Where do we go now?" Em asks.

"We're looking for a street called Ayuntamiento."

"Okay, let's get looking. Too bad we don't have Google Maps."

I laugh as I follow along behind Em.

Villa Ahumada is pretty run down. It's built on a grid, with lots of empty blocks that have returned to the desert surrounding us. People stare at us curiously—this was no tourist trap.

We stop in front of a brown, barnlike church where an old man is sitting on the railing out front.

"Hola," I say, struggling to remember the fragments of my Spanish. "¿Dónde rio Ayuntamiento?

He smiles and points over my shoulder. Confused, Em and I stared at each other, not sure what we should be looking for.

The old man points again, first behind us, then he sweeps his hand, tracing the street that we're on. "Estás aquí," he says. "Esta es la calle del Ayuntamiento."

We thank him and walk down the street. There's dust everywhere, and all the buildings are so shabby. Little kids run up to us and grab at our arms, begging for money. I wish I could give them something, but I didn't have anything I can spare. I don't know how long we will be on our own.

Wow, is all I can think. Back home I had a big house with my own room and bathroom, kitchen, clothes, and space. Many of these houses are just rusted metal shacks. I will never take anything for granted ever again.

Stop.

I stop next to an abandoned wooden shop that's listing badly to one side.

"That's it," I say. "This is why we're here."

"How do you know?" Em asks.

"I just have this feeling."

Em shrugs and turns to head into the abandoned shop. At this point I don't think she cares anymore; I think she just wants to stop walking. But this place feels familiar. It feels safe, almost like home.

"Watch out for scorpions," she murmurs, obviously not getting the same vibe.

We walk with our shoes crunching on broken glass that sparkles in the sunlight. Most of the roof has fallen away— it's too bright in here for a scorpion den, I think. Collapsed wooden beams hang like stalactites. Somehow it's even dustier in here than on the street. It appears as if no one has set foot inside this place in a long time.

"Are you sure this is why we're here?" Em asks. "We already had all the dirt we needed back in West Texas."

"I'm not sure about anything," I say, a little irritated. Doesn't she get that I'm as clueless and lost as she is? I've told her everything I know. "Let's keep looking and if there's nothing here we can just move on."

With each step we take the floorboards creak and puffs of dirt kick up. The wind howls through the gaps in the walls. I don't scare that often but this scene is too predictable. Next a zombie is going to come out and eat our brains.

"Hello? Is anyone here?" I ask. Nothing, of course.

"Look there's like a kitchen back here or something," Em says.

"Let's go check it out."

We walk through an empty doorway into the grossest kitchen I have ever seen. Countless ants crawl over a pot encrusted with dried stains and a pair of plates smeared with moldering food that's no longer recognizable.

Em laughs. "Well, that explains the awful smell."

It's good to hear her laugh. There hasn't been much of that lately.

"Wait, this food, it's not that old," I say. "Not if we can still smell it. Someone was here." Hope begins to resurface. "Maybe we just missed them."

"Yeah, maybe." Em turns away from me, and starts to trace some design on the wall. Wiping away only the first layer of dust. "How can we find something if we don't know what we're looking for? Maybe we should just get out of Mexico before the USI finds us."

"We don't have anywhere else to go."

Em doesn't answer. She still has her back to me as she retraces the design with her nails, marking their territory with a white line as the last layer of dust is scratched away.

"Okay, clearly something else is bothering you and I'm sorry," I say. "I'm so sorry you got dragged into this with me. I'm sorry that they're hunting you too. I'm sorry that we're standing in this putrid kitchen with no idea of where to go. I'm sorry I'm the worst best friend ever. I'm just so, so, sorry."

I'm crying now. Em slowly turns around. As she looks at me, I see all of our endless love and compassion. I head towards her reaching out my arms for a hug. Then with a groan followed by a loud crack the floor collapses and I fall screaming into the darkness.

The Sky Is Green

"PARIS! PARIS!" EM SHOUTS from up above. I want to call back and tell her that I'm alright, but I'm too stunned to answer. All the air has been knocked out of my body. When I can breathe again a huge wave of pain consumes me.

Snap out of it! I stand up on shaky legs. I look up at the light above. I'm not dying—that's just where I fell through the floor.

"I'm okay, Em," I finally manage to whisper. "I'm okay," I repeat in a stronger voice.

"Paris! Oh, thank goodness! Where are you? Can you make anything out?"

"It's too dark. I can't see a thing." I spin around. "What's that?" I swear I heard footsteps. "Em, I don't think I'm alone down here. I just heard something."

I start to back away from the noise when a light blinds me. I can't see anything for a couple seconds. Then I see the outline of someone standing in front of me—someone who is a lot bigger than me.

"Hello? Who are you?" I ask.

"She told me you would come. Hurry, bring your friend down here and follow me." It's an older man, from the sound of his voice. Raspy, low, way too mysterious for my liking.

"How do I do that? I don't see any stairs."

"Knock it off," he says. "She told me that you will have mastered telekinesis by now, so bring her down here." He turns and starts walking away.

"She told you? Who? My mom?"

"All your questions will be answered soon enough," he says, not turning or slowing his pace.

"Wait, please. I can't see without your light."

He turns around and shines the light in my direction. I hesitate before moving Em, but if my mom trusted this man enough to tell him about me then I guess I can try to trust him too.

"Okay, Em," I call up to her. Relax, I'm going to bring you down here." I gently lift her off the ground and slowly drop her through the floor until she's standing next to me.

"Who is that?" Em asks.

"I'm not sure. But he knows who I am, and he knows my mom."

Em grins. "Finally! Maybe we'll figure this out after all! This is like the worst scavenger hunt ever."

The stranger clears his throat. We follow him for a couple of minutes until we come to a big cement room. He flips the light on, revealing what appears to be his home. It's not exactly what I'd call charming. There's a small bed with a single pillow and a small blanket that I'm sure doesn't fit him, a little kitchen with a fridge, a small round wooden table with two matching wooden chairs, and an old-fashioned radio. Don't even get me started on the bathroom—there isn't one. Nope, just a tiny toilet, or should I say bucket in the corner. I'm not quite sure how that works, and I don't want to find out.

"Wow, it sure is cozy in here," I say. "Where is here exactly?"

"We're under the streets of Villa Ahumada," he says as if I'm dumb. He walks toward the fridge, but doesn't open it. Instead he just stands there, refusing to look me in the face.

"Right." Of course, because that clears everything up. "Okay, so can you answer some questions now?"

"No."

"Why not?"

"Because you're not ready."

"Look," I snapped, "I've been through a lot more than you think. I've fought tons of agents, I got shot in the arm, I had my heart broken, my dad—"

"She said you will be ready in the morning," he interrupts. "And she asked me to deliver a message." He turns around to face me, finally looking me directly in the eyes.

"Don't give up," he recites. "Don't have doubts. I'm sorry that this has happened to you without an explanation. I wish that I could be there for you. Trust the dreams. Don't jump to conclusions—instead show compassion for those who have hurt your heart. Learn to find peace, love, and joy in this journey. Cherish the time you spend with your best friend. Most importantly, I love you. I always have and I always will. Goodbye for now, but I will see you soon." he breaks eye contact and pivots back around as a single tear leaves my eye and floats down my cheek leaving a glossy trail behind it.

Silence follows as I dab my eyes.

How could she have known all of that? Gift or no gift, how could she? If she knew that I was going to be here at this exact time, why isn't she here to meet me? Why did she send us on a wild goose chase when she knew that we wouldn't find her?

She said to trust the dreams. If they're true and my mom knew exactly what was going to happen to me, then maybe she caused the dreams. But why didn't she give me this message in person?

"Thank you for delivering the message," Em says, interrupting my thoughts.

"Get some rest," the man says. "We will begin tomorrow."

Begin what? Whatever, I guess I'll find out tomorrow. Em and I pull the blankets from our backpack and lay them on the cold cement.

"Thank you, sir." Em says. "I'm sorry, but I don't think I ever caught your name."

"José Jalisco."

∞   ∞   ∞

I climb out of bed and stretch. When I turn around to smooth out the sheets, I see a teenaged boy lying there. I scream and he doesn't move. Another dream. I sit down and wait for something to happen. An hour passes, and then another. The wait is excruciating.

I've been sitting here for four hours when the alarm finally goes off. My mom, still in her famous pink, walks in to wake up her new replacement child. She gently shakes his shoulder until he opens his eyes. How is it that my mom can be a mother to all these girls and boys instead of me!

"Matt, it's time to wake up. We need to continue your training."

"Just ten more minutes, please," Matt begs.

"No. Time to go," my mom says.

Thank you, I think.

Matt moans and sits up. He shivers then follows my mom outside without saying a word. Isn't he going to eat? Or at least brush his teeth and change clothes? I guess not.

Once again they're living in a two-room wooden shed, but this one is hidden in a thick jungle. Just the tiniest flickers of sunlight slip through the canopy above. The most beautiful orchids I have ever seen in my life cling to the trees.

"Ready?" my mom asks.

"Ugh," Matt groans.

"Today you will learn how to become invisible."

That wakes him up. "Invisibility! Yes, I'm ready!"

"It's time to step things up," my mom says with a grin. "The key to invisibility is picturing and then almost erasing yourself. Invisibility is an enhancement of your perspective, your vision. It will come naturally or it will be one of the most challenging things you can do. To be invisible you have to feel invisible to the people who surround you."

Hmm. I guess I feel invisible to Camden—maybe I could use that.

"Okay, so what do I do?" Matt asks.

"I've already told you all that I can. This is why it is one of the hardest to master."

Matt closes his eyes. His hand starts to flicker in and out of sight.

"Focus, relax, believe in yourself," my mom says in her soothing voice. More of Matt starts to disappear, but he continues to flicker.

I wonder how long it will last? Are you just invisible or can you pass through things like I can in these dreams?

Well, I guess I'll find out when I get back to reality and try this for real.

"Once you've mastered this we can move on to turning other people invisible."

"What? No way! That's so cool!"

"There are a few catches though. For one, you have to be touching the person—or persons."

"So you can make more than one person invisible?"

"Yes, though it does drain your energy more than anything else we have learned so far. There are exercises that can help you to control the energy, preventing you from passing out. But that is very difficult to master."

"How do you do it?" Matt asks.

"The same way you turn yourself invisible. Hold onto them, create the same connection like hearing people's thoughts, but with your vision and your energy, then erase both of your bodies."

"Can I try that?"

"Not until you are very advanced. If you do something that you are not yet ready for, you could—"

∞   ∞   ∞

I jolted up on my blanket, wide awake. What? I've never left a dream without hearing everything important. Why now?

It's still pitch black in this concrete bunker. I lie back down on my blanket, close my eyes, and start to drift off into another deep sleep.

∞ ∞ ∞

"Wake up."

I moan. Who is being so loud?

"Wake up."

"Shut up" is more like it, but I sit up on my blanket and rub my back.

"You are ready now," José says.

"Ready for what?" I groan as Em stirs beside me.

"You are ready to hear a little bit more about your connection with your mother."

"What connection?"

"Don't play dumb," José says.

"You mean the dreams?"

"Yes, but there is so much more. Think beyond the obvious. Use your brain, figure it out."

Wow, super helpful. Well, I don't have to figure it out— not with the Gift.

I am not going to give you the answer. Look back at all the clues...

I look at José, a little startled. How did he know I would read his thoughts at that exact moment? How does he know the answers to my questions? Wait a minute—could he... What if he has the Gift as well?

"All those years ago, I saved your mother's life," José says. "And she saved mine."

"What happened?" I glance over at Em, who is still asleep. José nods to the table and we each take a seat.

"Years ago your mother and two fourteen-year-old boys were captured by the USI. They were held hostage for two weeks before they managed to escape. Your mother never fully explained how. She only said that the USI made a mistake that allowed the three of them to run through a wall and get out of there."

"Who were the two boys? How did they get through the wall?"

José gives me a long look. "Perhaps you could let me see whether I can tell a proper story. If I leave anything out, please feel free to ask your questions."

"Sorry, I won't interrupt again," I say.

"The USI is based in Dexter, New Mexico. That's some harsh territory. Deserts and then alkaline flats with not much water, and little of that drinkable. But somehow they made it the 350 kilometers on foot."

José stops and closes his eyes.

"I know that you've been through a lot, and I don't want to discount that…I was working as an agent for the Border Control when I found them in the desert…It's a miracle that they were still alive. One of the boys, Tristen, had no memory of what happened. The other, James, had been badly harmed by the USI. Both of your mother's arms were broken.

"I immediately knew that I needed to help them, and that they were sent to me for a reason. I earned your mother's trust by sneaking them into Mexico and bringing them here. If you're curious, this is a panic room where my family hid when the cartels sent their soldiers on sweeps through the town. The main entrance is down that hallway. There's a staircase leading to the street.

"Nikki was hesitant to explain at first, but eventually she told me about the Gift, the USI, you, everything. Once your Gift was activated your father was supposed to get you out of Utah and meet up with her in London. That plan would change."

"Why?"

"She saw into the future. She saw you here with me. And so I've been waiting here to help you."

"Did she say anything else?"

"Not much."

"And the boys, did they recover?"

"Physically, yes, though Tristen never recovered his memory, at least not while they were here. The most I ever heard out of him was a sweet little song, the last of his innocent childhood. 'The sky is green and the grass is blue, the trees are yellow and so is my pillow.'"

"My dad used to sing that to me at night."

"Your mother insisted on leaving as soon as the boys were ready. She was afraid that the USI would find us. Before she left I told her that I was dying. I had been diagnosed with a large cancerous tumor in my brain. She gave me a small treatment of the Gift as a thank you present for my generosity and said it should heal me. She was right. My tumor is gone and I'm healthy again."

"I have a question," I say.

"Go right ahead."

"When I tried to read your mind, how come your thoughts matched exactly to mine?"

"I don't know how to explain it other than I just knew," José says. "I don't have anything like your powers, but I believe that it has something to do with the injection of the Gift."

"What are you guys talking about?" Em asks.

I turn around to see Em sitting up on her blanket. I catch her up on everything that José just told me.

"Mr. Jalisco," I say, "I've been trying to figure out what you mean by connection between my mom and me. Do you mean when we were exposed simultaneously our brains coupled in a sort of amalgamation, which allows for telesthesia to occur at any time?"

José smiles. "Perhaps I'm flattering my English skills, but I don't think your friend understood that either."

"Right. I mean, since we were exposed at the same time our brains linked together. So now we can communicate without being near each other? Almost like we draw on each other's energy in times of struggle?"

"Your mom explained it a little bit differently but that's about what it is in a nutshell."

"I wonder if our link will grow stronger if I train with her more."

"Nowadays, anything is possible," José says. "It's a whole new world we're living in, and I'm grateful that your mother gave me a chance to see it."

"If an injection of the Gift healed your brain tumor," Em says, "Par, your mother has just revolutionized science. She's cured cancer! I wonder if the USI knows."

"I bet they're trying to weaponize it," I say. "Curing cancer doesn't seem like something they'd be interested in."

José nods.

My stomach growls. "I'm starving."

"I have some asadero and tortillas in the fridge," he says. "Nothing to cook it with, though."

"What's ..." Em begins.

"Asadero? It's not unlike mozzarella, though I like it much more. Made right here in Villa Ahumada, like all the best is."

"Thanks, but I think I'm going to go and get some fresh air. Em, you wait here, understand?"

"Whoa, why so serious all of the sudden?"

"I just don't want you to come looking for me, okay?" I say.

"When you get out to the street turn right and just keep walking," José says. "There's a line of food stalls about six blocks away. You can use the stairs, but the way you came in is faster."

"Thanks," I say.

"Are you sure this is safe?" Em asks. "I mean, we're hiding in this bunker for a reason, right?"

"No, it's not safe," José says. "But do you think you're going to change her mind?"

Em frowns as I roll my eyes and stand up from my chair, then shuffle down the dark tunnel through this underground nightmare. It gets lighter (and smellier) near the hole in the kitchen floor, though I keep stumbling on broken floorboards that have fallen to the cement. I lift myself through the hole and to level ground. There's still an awful smell of rotten food. I run out of the shop, stepping on the broken glass.

It's such a happy feeling to once again be outside—that day underground felt like a month.

I begin my stroll down the street. Maybe my mood's improved, but the town doesn't seem so desolate today. Many of the houses are painted in cheerful reds, blues, greens, and yellows. I pass a hardware store where two men laugh as they work on an old Dodge pickup truck out front. Maybe because I was upset and I didn't know what I was searching for, I blocked out everything good and saw only the sadness that I was overwhelmed with.

A man and a woman are walking toward me, laughing quietly as they eat the quesadillas they're carrying in their hands. For some reason it reminds me of another dream —the one where my parents were meeting every year on their anniversary. Was that real too? My parents were in contact all along and my mom never thought to come visit me? Why not?

I try to remember what they said. That I'd gain my powers when I turned eighteen, but I already know that. A secret! What secret? Something they thought I wasn't ready to handle. Something about Tristen. The same kid who the USI tortured along with my mom?

You would think that as the smartest person on the planet I wouldn't get stumped over stupid things like this. I can move things with my mind, and control other people's brains, but when it comes to looking at the bigger picture and connecting the dots I'm just a regular teenage girl. Though it was weird that I started talking about amalgamations and telesthesia back in the bunker. Maybe intelligence is part of the Gift as well. Hopefully I'll have another dream soon where I learn that.

As I turn north down the avenue with all the food stalls I see two men who seem out of place. One of them shows a vendor a photograph, and the man shakes his head. It's the USI. I turn back toward Calle Ayuntamiento and see four more USI agents questioning people on the street. The intersection has a dead end, so that gives me only one way to escape. But I count six USI agents to the south of me. One of them looks up at me and shouts. He collapses to the ground, blood spurting from his chest. The next five drop in as many seconds. I whirl back around and the agents north of me are running for their lives. Neither of them makes it. I run toward Ayuntamiento. Two of the agents are down and the other two are firing toward a rooftop to my right. A sniper!

The final two agents fall just seconds later. I stand up and run around the corner, sprinting south down the avenue. I stop as I see someone running toward me. Camden?

"Paris!" he shouts.

Someone pushes past me—a man holding a pistol. "Leave, it's not safe here," he says. He points the gun at Camden's head. Camden's boots scrape against the pavement as he halts his sprint. I glance back and forth between the man and Camden. I could let the man finish him off right now.

"Wait!" I shout. I may hate his guts, but I also love him. "Wait, don't shoot."

The man walks over to Camden and strikes him across the head with his gun. Camden collapses to the ground like all the bones have been sucked from his body.

"Who are you?" I ask.

"A friend. Now go." He starts hurrying down the avenue to the north.

I rush back to the cold gray cement prison where Em is pacing back and forth. There are tears in her eyes.

"I can't believe I let you go out there without me!" Em exclaims.

José eyes me. "I guess you weren't hungry after all. I was hoping you'd bring me back some guisado."

"About that..." I say. I tell them about the agents and the mysterious man who wiped them out. And how he knocked out Camden.

"Camden?" Em asks.

I nod.

"Par, I'm so sorry you had to see him but are you crazy! We are never splitting up again. Ever. Do you understand me?"

"Yes, ma'am."

"This isn't funny. You scared me to death!" Em stomps off. She won't stay mad for long. Fifteen minutes from now she will have forgotten why she was mad in the first place. Most girls can sit and hold a grudge for months. But Em, I think the longest time she's ever held a grudge was maybe thirty minutes, and that was for a very, very good reason.

I think it might be best to give her some time to herself to get over this. I turn back to José. I want to ask him if my mom ever mentioned a way to turn on—I don't know what to call it—I guess full access to problem solving. But he's staring at me with a look that silences me.

"Are you ready?" he asks.

Ugh, not again.

"Ready for what?"

He smiles. "Ready to continue your training, of course."

CHAPTER 8

Wanted

"TWO WEEKS. TWO WEEKS! Two freaking weeks and nothing. She's eighteen freaking years old. Eighteen! I give you one job to do. How hard could that be? She has no teacher, no friends, nothing—we made sure of that. How on earth could a dozen of my agents fail to bring in a teenage girl with no training, no development whatsoever of her Gift yet?"

"But sir—"

"No. You have lost the privilege to speak to me. You are a disgrace."

"Sir, forgive me, but she has had training. We were unprepared. And she wasn't alone."

"Emily Chase?" Terrence McCray spits. "What did she do—blind our men with a hairspray can?"

"I'm not talking about Em," Camden says. "There was someone else."

"And who might that have been?"

"Someone who wasn't afraid to kill. I don't know who he was. He sniped from a distance, everyone just started dropping."

"How is it that someone who is not afraid to kill all twelve of my men spares your life?" Terrence asks. The expression on "The Terror's" face as he leans in turns Camden white.

"I was standing with the other agents when they just started dropping. To my left, right, behind me, everywhere. The next thing I new everyone was down except for me. I don't know who it was, but Paris told him to spare me."

"Camden, it's your lucky day. Instead of killing you, I'm going to use you. Paris won't hurt you—badly, that is—so you can get close to her."

"Please, don't make me do this anymore. Please, just let me go."

"You're free to go at any time," the director of the USI says with a smirk. "Jackson, however—he and I are becoming better friends, and he'll be staying."

"He's just a kid!" Camden yells, staring Terrence down. "I'm going to expose you. I'm going to go divulge your secrets to the CIA. I'm going to tell them everything!"

Terrence laughs. "No, you're not. If you did, Jackson might have an unfortunate accident. And we both know how unpleasant some accidents can be."

Camden drops his head. "What are my orders, sir?"

"You are to stay here until your leg heals, and help locate Paris. Dismissed."

Camden walks out the door and down the spare gray hallways of the USI's New Mexico base. New corridors break off at random and at all angles, making it impossible to stay oriented. The facility is a giant maze, which only adds to the helplessness and despair that makes this place so depressing.

After a few wrong turns Camden eventually finds his room, which he shares with fifteen other boys. All of them are being held hostage here in some way or another. Terror is an emotion that most people do not have to face. These boys have to look terror in their eyes every day and Camden is sure they will soon reach a point where they cannot take it anymore.

∞   ∞   ∞

"Start preparing the jet," Terrance says. "I'm taking a team to London in three days."

The agent raises his eyebrows. "London, sir?"

"You think they're going to just wait for us in Mexico, you dolt? Once we find their new location we'll send a team. As for now I have business in London."

"Your physician recommended that you stay here to recuperate from your injuries in Fishlake."

"There's no time," Terrance snaps. "An asset sent us a tip that Nikki Taylor is in London, and our agents have confirmed it. We know where she's hiding but she won't stay long. Now get out of here."

Terrence waits for the door to close and then starts pacing back and forth in his office. Who's the man who saved Paris Taylor's life? Her father? He showed no sign of the Gift while he was detained, but he did just somehow manage to escape.

Paris is still the key, not her mother. Well, we need to bring Nikki in too because she's dangerous, but there's something different about her daughter.

"What if it was Ryker?" he says. "There's no one else it could have been. No one else has the skills or the ruthlessness to kill a dozen of my agents. Ryker, of course!"

Ryker was the best black ops agent anyone had ever seen. He successfully completed more missions than any other operative in the USI. In the summer of 2002 Ryker was asked to infiltrate Cumberland, Maine, and investigate rumors that his ex-partner Maverick was living there. It was said that Maverick's wife was conducting research that could endanger innocent civilians. Ryker refused and resigned his commission. Unwilling to lose his best man, Terrence had Ryker brainwashed, wiping his memory, and rebuilding his ethics from scratch. Ryker wasn't the same after that. Some missions he completed perfectly; on others he went on rampages that were difficult to clean up. His final mission was to bring in Nikki Taylor and her two prodigies. At some point he snapped, allowing the three of them to escape. He disappeared after that.

Terrence presses the intercom. "I want everyone in Conference Room 3-16B in ten minutes."

∞ ∞ ∞

The base turns into a madhouse as agents stampede toward the conference room. Camden strolls behind his roommates, overwhelmed with disgust. He's no longer afraid of what Terrence will do to him, because he knows that Terrence needs him alive. He's the only one who can get close to Paris.

He walks into the conference room and takes a seat in the back row. There are hundreds of technicians, clinicians, soldiers, agents, and officers sitting in dead silence. Terrence is standing behind the podium on the dais at the front of the room.

"We are going to address the issue of Paris Taylor." Terrence pauses, waiting for the whispers to die down. "Paris Taylor is a dangerous, unstable fugitive who needs to be brought in. She, like her mother Nikki Taylor, has been exposed to the Gift. Her father, Maverick Taylor, escaped from our custody several days ago in the midst of a transport. Acquiring him is of tertiary concern because we have determined that he has not acquired the Gift.

"Apprehending those who have been exposed to this bioengineering monstrosity has become the sole mission of the USI. Governments around the world are beginning to question our effectiveness and are considering defunding us in favor of their own agencies. We cannot let that happen or this agency, which has worked in the shadows to the benefit of billions over the past decades, will be dissolved.

"The majority of the people in this room will receive a new assignment regarding Paris Taylor. I warn you now, do not underestimate her skills despite her lack of training. Others have in the past. And to compound things, Ryker has resurfaced. He eliminated a dozen of our agents who were trying to apprehend our target in northern Mexico."

The room hums with barely suppressed shock and dismay.

"Paris Taylor had crossed the border despite lacking a passport. After interrogating the Border Patrol agent responsible, we have determined that she's gained the ability to control minds."

More murmuring.

"However, our scientists have developed a chip that will protect you from this aspect of the Gift. Once it's implanted above the ear, no one can subject you to any mind reading or control. Currently the chip lasts for twenty-four hours before it needs to be replaced.

"Paris Taylor must be found. She is only a child and is bound to make a mistake. Find her and bring her in—dead or alive."

The murmurs turn to a dull roar of frantic whispers as Terrence exits the room.

Camden stays seated as the others file out. How can he find a way out of this? If he doesn't help bring Paris in,

Jackson will suffer instead. How can he choose one over the other?

Several minutes pass as Camden sits with his face in his hands. Trapped inside of an organization that had ordered its agents to murder an eighteen-year-old American citizen who had never committed a crime. How could they get away with this?

Maybe that was the answer—go beyond the USI? Maybe it doesn't reach to the top. But how to find out?

Camden stands up and starts pacing back and forth across the room. A risky idea pops into his head. On the base there is a tech room known as "All Knowledge"—or at least that's what his roommates called it.

He quickly exits the room, almost running, hoping that he can find some answers. Once he reaches the room he swipes his access card. Denied. Camden decides to wait until someone enters or leaves—then he'll sneak in behind them.

Hours pass before finally a woman opens the door, reaches back to turn off the lights, and walks away. Camden slides his foot into the doorway, waits for the woman to round the corner, then slips through the door and turns back on the light.

Once inside, he can't believe what he's seeing. The room is as big as a warehouse. Rifles in all shapes and sizes hang on racks lining one wall. On the opposite side, an endless row of cabinets that stretch to the ceiling. He opens a few shelves—each is stacked with computer chips, handheld and wearable devices that he can't recognize, goggles for some unknowable purpose ... A fleet of black sedans is parked at the far end of the space, and row after row of computers fill the center.

Camden pulls up a seat, logs in, and searches "USI." Hundreds of websites stream in.

The first site listed reads: "The Unknown Secret Intelligence: A secret global organization with a mandate to stop world threats that the people are not ready to know about. Sponsored by many countries including: Germany, Italy, France, Russia, UK, US, Iceland, North Korea, India, China, and Japan. The USI has authority to do whatsoever they see fit to ensure the safety of the world."

The second site reads: "The USI was founded in 1948 after scientists began experimenting on human subjects in an attempt to grant them inhuman strength. Involuntary participants began disappearing all over the world. None are believed to have survived. The USI was founded to protect innocent lives from these perversions at all costs. More than 120 countries have given the USI their full support, resulting in the establishment of more than one hundred bases around the world."

Camden leaned back in his chair and stared at the ceiling far above. This is bigger than me, he thought. This is bigger than Jackson.

CHAPTER 9

Lost and Found

TRAINING. FINALLY. "Yes, I'm 100% ready to officially start my training."

José's smirk widens. What's so funny?

"Follow me," he says, pulling open a concealed door hidden in the gloom.

I blindly follow him down a narrow dark hallway, unsure of where I'm going or what lies ahead. I guess I just have to trust him. José stops and opens a second door. He reaches in and flips on a light switch, spilling a thin puddle of light into the hallway.

"It's going to take forever to find it."

I follow him into the empty room. "Find what? Can I help you look?"

"No. You're not supposed to know until you're ready."

I throw up my hands. "Fine. I'm done. I'm not going to sit around and have a stranger who doesn't know the slightest thing about me control my life, my training, anything. No, you're not ready to be my trainer. I don't need you. I can do this on my own." I stomp away toward the door.

"Now you're ready," José says.

Ugh, dumb mind tricks. I stop, refusing to turn back around, slowing my breathing and focusing on all the sounds around me. Maybe I can hear his heart and tell if he's lying. Nothing. Well, that would have been cool. Maybe someday.

"You can move forward in your next step of training because you finally have confidence in yourself. Your mother was very clear that this is what you must master during your time here. Now that you have done this, you can help me find what I am missing and I will attempt to train you. The first thing we will work on is focusing."

Are you kidding me? My skill level is way beyond that.

"To be able to focus is extremely important because when you put your mind to something and concentrate, you can accomplish anything. It's the foundation of the Gift."

You know, this time I'm just gonna go with it. "So what is it that we're looking for?"

"Your mother's journal," José says. "She recorded her training regimen and what happened while she stayed here. There was also a section of notes on how I can help you." He starts rummaging through the trash sloping down from one corner of the room.

"She told me that when the time came I would find it and not to worry…" he says, distracted by his search. "I still don't understand it."

Who does? I for sure as heck don't.

"Well then, I guess we just get to look until we stumble upon it." I walk over to a jumbled stack of boxes in the corner of the room, opening them up and searching through them. It's going to take a while to search every inch of this room—you could fit five cars in here. Splintered wood lies in piles, interspersed with chunks of crumbling concrete. More boxes loom in the right back corner, while large rocks and a stack of wood fill the far-left corner.

I wonder how José can even teach me—he doesn't have the Gift. Well, he kinda doesn't have it. He has so much junk in these boxes. What's the point of it all? There's old stuffed animals, hairbrushes, ripped blankets, soiled clothes, notebooks, toy trucks and cars …

"What's all this stuff for?" I ask.

"This is what I collected for your mother and the two boys while they were staying here," José says. He stares at the wall with sad eyes.

"I don't think the journal's here," he says after a moment. "It's too obvious."

"I think that's exactly why it might be in here," I say. "The best hiding spot is right under your nose."

"You might be right. Nikki was always playing mind tricks."

I stand up and try to think. If I was my mom, where would I hide the journal? Problem is, I don't know anything about my mom. But maybe she's like me—where would I hide it?

I scan the room. I wouldn't hide it in the broken wood and concrete; it could get damaged. I'd probably put it in the wall if I had the power to pass through solid objects. The problem is that I don't, at least not yet. I start knocking on the walls, looking for a hollow spot.

"That's smart," José says.

Smart? I don't think so. Desperate, maybe. But I thank him anyway.

Thirty minutes pass as I run my hand over almost every inch of the four walls. I'm ready to give up. My hands are cramping and my knuckles are swollen. Wow, I have really weak hands. I wonder if we're even looking in the right room. Why not the bunker? Is there really a journal? Because it sure doesn't seem like it.

I look at the boxes again. Did I check behind them? I can't remember. I slide the boxes away from the wall. When I go to knock, I stumble forward as my hand passes through the darkness. There's a hole in the wall! I reach in deeper and feel around till I touch something that might be leather. I close my eyes and pull.

"I found it!" I shout, jumping up and down. "It is real!"

José leans over my shoulder as I flip open the first page. I can't take my eyes off of what I'm seeing. José impatiently tries to turn the page and I swat his hand away. Just two words, but they mean everything to me: "For Paris."

After taking a moment to compose myself I turn the page to a list of notes after notes on how to help me train, what to teach me, even what I need to be told.

"Okay, let's get started," José says. He pulls on the journal and I grudgingly let go. "Let's start with a review so you can show me how much you know, and we can take it from there." He gestures toward the pile of broken wood and rocks in the far left corner.

I pick up a piece of broken concrete with the Gift, move it across the room, then set it back down.

"Good, now pick up everything in that pile," José says.

I stare at him in disbelief.

"A master of telekinesis could do it, and more."

"Well, I can't."

"Then pick up what you can."

Okay, I'll try. I focus all of my energy on picking up everything in the pile. At first nothing happens, then gradually the pile begins to hover off the ground.

"Lift it higher."

Higher? Sweat drips down my face, but I keep pushing. One foot off the ground, two, three…everything comes crashing down to the ground. I drop to my knees, exhausted. I've never felt like this before.

"Okay, what did you think?" I gasp.

"What you just did was very impressive for someone who is new to this. Nikki wrote down different levels of skill that we can base your training on. A starting point. It contains a table that includes the skill level, what you should be able to accomplish in that level, and how long you should be training to reach the next level. From what I can see so far it looks like you're going to fall into the strong intermediate."

I scowl.

"That's not so bad," he says. "Most intermediates will have trained for a couple of years."

Meanwhile my mom's been training for fifteen years. I can't imagine what she can do. Can she predict the future, control crowds, or even teleport?

"So now what?" I ask.

"Now we work on conserving energy."

"Here," José says, walking over and handing me the journal. "I think you can do this on your own. But I'll stick around in case you have any questions."

On my own? Maybe that could work, since it's really my mom teaching me through the journal.

"Okay, I'll try." I flip through the pages, just looking at her handwriting. It's nothing like mine. Hers is messy and hard to read as if she'd been writing in a hurry.

I turn to the intermediate section. José was right—I think this is where I'm at, skill wise. The first thing she says to do is clear my mind. The journal continues, "Close your eyes, relax, and try to visualize the energy surging through your body. Pick a color for the energy to be. Visualize it going from your brain to your toes and back.

Visualize the immense amount of energy coming from your brain. Instead of letting the energy all converge there, spread it throughout your body. Don't let any one spot have too much energy or it can overload your system. The body is not meant for the amount of knowledge and energy you now have, so the energy can never focus at one signal point or it could kill you."

Wow, isn't that reassuring. I close my eyes, but it's not working. I've never been good at visualization, and I don't know how it's going to work now. But I need to master this. Focus.

What else did my mom say? "It takes a large amount of focus." Well, no duh. "You have to believe in yourself. If you can believe in yourself anything is possible. It's the simple principle of dream, believe, create."

Dream, believe, create. I can do this. I already have the first one down, and half of the second. I close my eyes again, picturing my body. Pick a color. Okay, blue.

I begin to see what she's talking about. A blue current flowing. The neural impulses in my brain glow brightly. Each synapse becomes filled with transmitters, creating small glowing powerhouses throughout my body. I imagine some of the blue light leaving my brain and spreading through my body until everything is equal. I feel an overwhelming sensation of relaxation, peace, and strength. My body no longer feels weak in comparison to the Gift. There's no longer a division. My body and the Gift are now one, working together to give me strength. I stand in silence, simply enjoying the sensation.

"Have you made any progress?"

Startled, I open my eyes to see José watching me.

"Yes, more than I imagined was possible." I pause, taking a moment to reflect on what I accomplished. This is going to change my life.

"Maybe that's enough for one day then?" he asks, stifling a yawn.

"But I just got started."

José smiles. "Maybe so, but it's three in the morning."

"How is that possible," I ask. "We just got here."

"You started reading the journal and then you went into some kind of trance. You'd still be staring at nothing if I hadn't broken you out of it."

I wasn't in a trance. I was just…well, I don't know what. We got down here at about ten o'clock this morning. That's a full seventeen hours.

"How's Em?" I ask.

"She's fine. She's been catching up on her sleep. Her body needed it."

"Actually, there's no such thing as catching—"

"There's something else I need to tell you," José interrupts. "Get some rest now, and then you will need to leave in the morning. Your mother said you could not be here longer than two days." He twists his mouth to one corner. "I don't want you to feel like I'm kicking you out."

"No, I would never think that. I completely understand."

We look at each other—an awkward moment. He's a lot nicer than he seemed at first, and I'll miss him.

"Well, did she say where I should go?"

"Yes, she wants you to fly to London. I have an address for you there. She said that's where you will finally get all the answers you have been looking for." He smiles. "And perhaps you'll see her there."

"I don't understand. Why didn't I just go to London in the first place?"

"Because there were lessons you needed to learn. Things that you needed to learn by yourself instead of her just telling you what to think and how to act."

He makes a good point. I did learn what I'm capable of, the importance of my friendship, how fortunate I am to have a family and money and people who care about me. And I learned to accept the Gift and see it is a strength and not a weakness. Regardless, I wish I wasn't a pawn in my mother's game, tossed and turned like a doll.

∞   ∞   ∞

"Paris wake up."

"No…" I moan.

"We have to go." My brain finally registers what is being said and who's saying it.

"Em?"

"Yes."

"What time is it?" If she says anything before eleven I'm going to be mad.

"It's around noon."

Phew, that's more like it. My eyes scan the room unaware of what they're searching for till they find it. Well, him. José is sitting at the table and eating a tortilla and cheese sandwich. I refuse to call them quesadillas if they're not heated up.

"We wanted you to get as much sleep as possible," Em says, "but we're now in a time crunch and we need to get moving."

"What's the hurry?" I ask.

"I want to do a little sightseeing before we leave. Seriously, though, our flight out of Ciudad Juarez is at 6:30."

After a quick clean up we hug José goodbye and thank him for everything he has done for us. I sling the backpack with the journal over my shoulder and hug him again.

"Good luck," he says.

Em and I walk to the avenue with the food stalls and after a quick meal of burritos rolled around a deshebrada stew (José's recommendation), I "convince" some poor man to drive us to the airport outside of Ciudad Juarez. The traffic gets crazy, and it's past 5:30 when our driver drops us off at the departures zone. I give him $200 for his trouble.

"Perfect timing, my phone just died," Em says.

During the drive through the desert I debated how I was going to get us on the plane without a passport. I thought about convincing the ticket agent to sell us tickets without them, but I wasn't sure their software would allow that. And even if it did, that might tip off the USI. So straight to the security line it is.

"Are you feeling good enough to do this?" Em asks.

"Yep, all set." I've been practicing this for a while and I think I can do it, especially after the car ride here. I had our driver singing along with Em within the first ten minutes.

The line at security is an hour long so I grab a policeman and ask him to let us through. He does exactly as he's told and I feel a flush of pride. One of the security officers raises a fuss when my backpack with the cash passes through the scanner, but I convince him that they're actually just stacks of notecards. We walk to our gate, an Aeromexico flight with a connection in Mexico City. We won't get to London till 3:55 P.M. the next day.

When it's time to board, I tell Em to wait for everyone to go in before us. "We're flying first class," I whisper.

"Disculpe," the attendant says as we start down the jetway. "Sus boletos, por favor."

I smile and give her a little mental push. She smiles back and waves us on. "¡Tener un gran vuelo!"

We find two empty seats in first class after I convince the attendants on board to let us through. "We made it! Told you we would," I bragged to Em as we sit down.

Our transfer at Mexico City goes just as smoothly, and soon we're on our way to London. Em and I are practically jumping up and down in our seats when the attendant brings us our menus. We decline the champagne, and after a cheese plate, a smoked salmon appetizer with pico de gallo, and a spinach pasta for me and short ribs for Em, we dig into our cheesecake and watch a movie until we fall asleep.

∞   ∞   ∞

Terrence paces back and forth, staring at a giant door and waiting for it to open. I walk up to him, about to ask a question until I remember it's just another one of my mom's memories—I'm not actually here. But whose memory? This must be what José told me about, when she was captured. My stomach twists—I can't bear to see her tortured.

The enormous black door begins to lower into the floor. On the other side are two boys wrapped in chains with four men dragging them by each arm. Both boys are hunched over, unconscious. Six more men carry my unconscious mom beside them. A seventh man walks beside my mother. He's rolling a wheeled IV that's injecting some kind of fluid into her arm. A sedative? Something to block the Gift? Leading the group is the task force's commanding officer or whatever you call him. He looks just like the man who saved me in Villa Ahumada, extremely confident. Also very attractive and buff. Dreamy brown eyes with silky brown hair, reminds me a little of my dad.

"Ryker, report," Terrence demands.

"The mission went as planned," the leader says. "No distractions. No problems."

"Good. That is what I expect every time I give an order. Do you understand?" Terrence stares hard at Ryker, who simply nods in response. "Take the boys to the basement cells and Taylor to Interrogation. I want to know everything about this so-called gift—how it was developed, how it affects her, what she's capable of. Everything."

Ryker nods, and the four men drag the boys out of the room. I start to follow them but my vision goes foggy. I turn around and see that my mom is being carried in the opposite direction. I guess since it's my mom's memory I'm going to have to follow her. That's frustrating because I want to know more about those two boys. Who are they? How do they know my mom?

The next thing I know I'm standing right next to my mom, who is lying on a table strapped down in restraints. I must have wandered too far away from her so I was flashed here.

Ryker, the only other person in the room, is preparing some sort of injection. Once he completes it he walks over to my mom and injects it into her chest. Instantly she wakes up and struggles against her restraints. After a moment she calms down and asks, "What do you want?"

"I want to know everything," Ryker says, repeating what Terrence ordered.

My mom closes her eyes.

"Okay, we'll do this the hard way," Ryker says with a slight grin.

Ryker wheels over a tray of tools. I close my eyes, plug my ears, turn around, and walk as far away as I can from his table. Scream after scream pierces my ears. Why would a USI agent capable of this save me?

"This way," Terrence orders, pulling a boy by his arm. I don't know where I am now but I'm glad to be away from the torture. Terrence drags the boy around a corner and stops in front of a door.

"You need to cooperate unless you want this to be your future," Terrence says. He pushes the door open and inside my mom and the two boys are chained up against the wall. One boy is unharmed—it must be Tristen—while James and my mom were almost unrecognizable, every inch of their body covered in bleeding cuts. I gasp. How could they? How could they do that to a fourteen-year-old boy?

"I want to go home!" the other boy shouts at Terrence.

"Another word and that will be you." Terrence grins again as the little boy's face is overcome by fear. "Jackson, your family ..."

"No!" I shout at Terrence over and over again. I know that he can't hear me, but I need to say it. "You can't get away with this! You can't torture people! You can't just do what you want without consequences! No!"

∞   ∞   ∞

I jerk upright in my seat. "That can't be real. That can't be real," I whisper over and over. My face is wet with tears.

"Hmm?" Em says, stretching as she wakes up.

"I just had another dream ... and, well, this one I'm never going to be able to forget."

"What happened?"

"It was my mom, James, and Tristen, and a little boy who they called Jackson. The USI tortured them, did experiments on them. And they made Jackson watch. He was only like five years old."

I look out the window, staring at the profound blue ocean that comes to an end near the horizon.

"That's Ireland, I think," Em says. "Won't be much longer now. Have you decided what we're going to do when we land?"

I shrug. "I guess we'll just take a taxi to the address José gave us."

"Do you think it's safe?"

I shrug again. "It's a little late now. Unless you want to turn around and make that trip to New York after all."

Despite trying to sound confident, something isn't sitting right. I can't quite put my finger on it.

"Okay, what do we do once we get there?" Em asks.

"I don't know. I think we're going to have to wait and see."

"But your mom gave José that address—what, like seven years ago? What if things have changed?"

"Then we'll improvise like we always have," I snap.

We sit in silence until an attendant comes by and tell us that we've begun our descent into Heathrow. My ears pop and then I start gripping the armrests as the landing gear drops, slightly shaking the plane as it lowers. I've always been a nervous flyer.

Despite myself I look out the window and watch England expand as it rises up to meet us. At the last moment I close my eyes and the wheels touch down on the runway.

The pilot announces our arrival in Spanish and then again in English as we taxi to our gate. "Ladies and gentlemen, welcome to London. It is 4:02 in the afternoon with clear skies and a temperature of 11°C. Thank you for flying Aeromexico."

"I'm hungry," Em says.

CHAPTER 10

Pie in the Sky

IT'S GETTING LATE but I'm in no hurry to check out the address that José gave us, so I ask our taxi driver to drop us off about a mile south of it. It turns out that's in Notting Hill, and Em and I are blown away by how fun and charming it is. There are cute little parks and shops all over the place.

We roam the streets, searching for some kind of food that will satisfy both our cravings. A small shop catches our eye—a bakery called "Pie in the Sky" that serves breakfast sweets all day. Yes, sweets are exactly what I need, and that waiter sure is sweet looking. No words describe him other than "gorgeous" and "wow."

"Umm, hawt!" Emily exclaims. "Maybe we can make a friend?" The door chimes as Em pushes it open, wide eyed and ready to flirt.

"Hi, my name's James," the waiter says. "Will it just be the two of you?"

"Yes," I say.

James nods. "Perfect. Please follow me."

"Dibs," I whisper to Em.

"No way!" Em says.

"Come on, I need to get over Camden."

"No, no, no, you are not using Camden as an excuse. You can rebound with someone else."

"Okay, then we let him pick," I say. "That's only fair."

"Ugh, fine, but I'm going to win."

"We'll see about—"

"Here we are," James says. "I'll be back in a couple minutes to take your order."

"Thank you!" both Em and I say at the same time, desperate in competition. James smiles and walks away. We sit at a cute little table for two against the window looking out at the street. A classic cafe filled with beautiful wooden furniture and overwhelming coziness.

Em and I study our menus. Pancakes sound really good right now. Ooh, crepes, that sounds amazing.

"Alright ladies, are you ready to order?" James asks with a beaming smile.

"Yes, I would love the strawberry crème crepes please," I say while getting lost in his beautiful blue eyes.

"And I would love the pancake platter, thank you," Em says, batting her eyelashes. We're like two shopaholics fighting over a scarf.

"My pleasure," James says as we hand him our menus. Em and I wait for him to reach a safe distance before both our faces drop in awe.

"Honestly, so freaking cute. Please just let me have him," I beg.

"No way. You just got out of a serious relationship so it's my turn."

"Exactly, I just got out of my relationship and I need to get over Camden. It's perfect."

"He's too pretty to be a rebound. Didn't we just have this conversation like ten minutes ago?" Em asks.

"Well yes, but I just love the topic." We break out in laughter. It's nice to just sit here and have girl talk. For the first time in forever we're just normal teenage girls flirting with the waiter.

James returns with our food. Steam rises from our plates, yes! Fresh off the griddle. He asks if we need anything else, then continues on to another table.

Oh my gosh. Nutella, strawberries, powdered sugar, and bananas all folded up inside four perfect triangles. Chocolate sauce drizzled on top along with sprinkles of sugar, strawberry sauce, and a mountain of whipped cream. Beautifully elegant, but most importantly, delicious.

While eating Em and I talk and talk about random stuff that has no importance. I confess my Ed Sheeran prank and she pokes my arm with her fork. Then our laughter is cut short by an explosion.

"What was that?" Em asks.

"I don't know, but it sounded bad. Somewhere down that street."

Em looks at me, and I realize what she's thinking. That's in the direction of the address José gave us. But how could the USI know that we're here already?

"Let's go check it out," I say, jumping up and leaving cash on the table. We quickly exit the cafe in a hurry down the street, pushing through crowds of people who are running in the opposite direction.

Em grabs my arm. "Paris, if that was the USI, we can't just charge straight into this."

"I'll handle it," I say.

"How can you be sure?"

"I'm not," I say, then take off running again. We cautiously peer around the corner down Stoneleigh Place. There is debris all over the street in front of a charred house.

I grab Em and we duck back behind the corner. "That has to be our house."

"How can you tell?"

I reach up and point to the officers on site. "They've got to be USI."

"How could they have gotten here so fast?" Em asks.

"Maybe they were waiting for us," I say. "Who knows?"

"I hope no one was inside." Em says.

"They're not going to get my mom that easily. But we've got to get out of here."

"Why don't you read their minds first?"

That's smart—why didn't I think of that? I focus all of my attention on trying to read one of the agents' minds.

Nothing. I direct my attention to another agent, then another, and another—still nothing.

"Em, I think we might have a problem. I can't read their minds."

"That's not good," Em says.

"I know." If I can't read their minds, will nothing work? I want to try lifting them, but that would tip them off.

"I think we might have another problem," Em says. "Terrence."

It looks like Terrence is still pretty banged up from the beating I gave him. His face is badly bruised, and he walks with a limp.

"What are those things on their temples?" Em asks.

"What things?"

"I don't know—that's why I'm asking."

I study the man closest to us. It looks like some sort of gray or black disk. Maybe an anti-Gift implant? I need to get one so I can see what it really does, but that will have to wait.

"So I don't think there's anything we can do right now," I say. "Let's get a hotel and try to think things through."

"Maybe James can recommend one," Em says.

I don't have any better ideas, so we turn and head back to the café, where James is locking up. He looks at us and smiles. "You two again. What's up?"

Em bats her eyelashes. "We were just wondering what's fun to do around here. A handsome guy like you must know a lot of places."

As Em flirts I try to read James's mind. Nothing! Is he USI too? Have I lost my power somehow? No, I can hear Em marveling at his body. There's no implant on either of his temples. So how is he blocking the Gift? I decide to take a chance, and before I can stop myself I say—

"Excuse me, James, but does the name Nikki Taylor mean anything to you?"

His face tenses at the mention of her name. "No, sorry. Should it?"

"Have you ever heard of an organization called the USI?" Again his face tenses, he has to be hiding something.

"No, I'm sorry again," James says. "I've never heard of the USI."

"I think you're lying."

"Who are you?"

If he was with the USI then he would have made a move by now. Which means he either has no idea about any of this and I'm just some crazy person—or he's the James who my mother took care of. Someone I might be able to trust. Well, here goes nothing.

"My name is Paris. Paris Taylor."

The confusion on his face shifts to fear.

"Follow me," he says, unlocking the door and ushering us in.

"What are you doing?" Em whispers into my ear.

"There's only one of him. I could take him."

"Where are we going?" Em asks as we follow James into the kitchen.

"Somewhere we can talk," James says. He leads us out the back of the building and down an alley to the next street over. He takes the keys out of his pocket and a silver Tesla parked on the curb beeps. "Get in."

I've been trusting my gut but this is as far as my gut is taking me. "No, sorry," I say. "I don't trust you."

"Please, we're not safe here."

"No." I state.

James scowls at me. "What else do you want me to do? I can't tell you anything here."

"Paris, maybe we should just go." Em says.

"I don't trust him yet."

"If I were USI those agents on Stoneleigh would be all over you by now," James snaps. "But I'm not so let's go."

Okay, so it is him. I climb into the car.

∞   ∞   ∞

After a long drive to the suburbs of London, we're sitting in a room that reminds me of Mexico. What's with all the underground prisons? Concrete walls, unpainted. Two beds on opposite sides of the room, a small couch, a mini fridge, and a round dinner table with three chairs. Their "rabbit hole," as James explained. He introduced us to Tristen when we arrived.

"So where's my mom?" I ask.

"There was an emergency that she had to attend to," Tristen says. "But she should be back in a couple of weeks. She asked me to apologize for her."

I lean back in my chair and close my eyes. So this is the end of our wild goose chase.

"So you have the Gift." Tristen says.

"Yep."

"And you know how to use it?"

"Well, kinda. Not really." I glance around the room. "So we're stuck down here together for a couple weeks?"

"Unfortunately," James says.

"What's your problem?" I snap.

"I don't have one," he snaps back.

"So, tell us about yourselves," Tristen says. "We might as well pass the time with some conversation.

Em and I dive into our past while James makes dinner. Telling Tristen all about our likes, dislikes, school, families, and past relationships while reliving our best memories. Em talks the most—she's clearly shifted her interest from James to my mom's other ward.

"I don't mean to interrupt, but let me help James finish up with dinner," Tristen says.

I lean back on the couch next to Em, who can't take her eyes off of Tristen. "Someone has a crush," I tease.

"I think it's way more than a crush. He's so sweet and considerate. I just want to run my fingers through his choppy blonde hair. He looks a little bit like you, actually."

I laugh, then give her a push. "Go help him."

"You think I should?" Em asks.

"Of course! He likes you too."

"Are you sure?"

"Well, I don't know. But I think so."

"Oh, could you find out?" Em asks, fluttering her eyes.

"Fine."

"Thank you, you're the best! ...Well?"

"You're all he was thinking about. So get your cute butt over there!" I say, smacking her on the rear as she stands up.

Em's face lights up with a giant grin as she walks across the room and asks Tristen if there's anything she can do to help. Tristen really is very good looking. He's tall, thin yet built, with short blonde hair on the sides and longer on top and a very defined jaw, but for some reason I'm not attracted to him at all. He feels more like a close friend even though we just met. Actually, he somewhat reminds me of Camden and James except that James has brown hair and eyes.

I watch as Em and Tristen flirt like crazy while we eat. They already seem so close, as if they've known each other for years.

"Great, this makes things even worse," James says in a conspiratorial tone.

"Excuse me?" I ask.

"With Tristen and Emily acting all lovey dovey I'll be stuck talking to you for the next few weeks."

"What's with all of the attitude?"

"I have attitude? Excuse me, know it all, but you're the privileged brat who's had the perfect life. You expect everything to go your way and boss people around."

"You know nothing about me," I snap. "Look, we're in this together, so why are you pushing me away?"

"We're not in this together. I've been on the run my entire life. I can't remember a time where I wasn't constantly checking over my shoulder. I don't even know what my real name is."

"James I'm—"

"That safe house that blew up was my home for seven years. And it was beginning to feel like home. But none of that matters anymore because it's gone. Everything's gone. They know where we are and now we're going to have to disappear again. I've started over too many times. I don't want to do it again."

I reach out and touch his hand. "I'm going to help you get through this, I promise."

I look up at Em and Tristen, but they don't appear to have heard a word we've said. Em is too busy telling him about her cheerleading days.

"James, how come I can't read your mind?" I ask.

He gives me a flirtatious smile. "Trying to read my mind? Was there something in particular you would like to know?" His mood swings are going to give me whiplash.

"No, I just, I—"

"Trust goes both ways. I don't trust you yet."

I roll my eyes as dramatically as possible. "For a second there I thought we might actually become good friends."

"Oh, Paris, where's the fun in that?" James teases.

Why is it that I'm beginning to hate him with every bone in my body but at the same time I get butterflies every time he says my name? How can someone be so mature but at the same time act like a child?

After dinner Em and I climb into our bed, exhausted. I have no way to tell time down here. No sun to wake us up in the morning or stars to shine at night. I'm out the second my head hits the pillow.

∞ ∞ ∞

A week has passed. Em and Tristen are inseparable, always holding hands, cuddling, talking, and kissing. If I didn't know better I would have thought they were on their honeymoon.

Things with James and I are a bit more complicated. We flirt constantly in the form of friendly arguing. I think we secretly both like each other but we're too stubborn to admit it or make the first move. We've gotten to know almost everything there is to know about each other except for how he blocks the Gift.

"What's your favorite movie?" I ask, sinking into the couch next to him. He slides his arm around me and stares into my eyes.

"Impossible," he says. "There's too many good movies."

"Okay, top three."

"Sorry, still can't do it."

I shrug off his arm. "You're no fun."

"Well, what about you? What's your top three?"

"Umm, anything Marvel. And the Fast and Furious series. Oh, and I love Harry Potter and Star Wars and Lord of the Rings. I'm a sucker for chick flicks too, like The Notebook or The Holiday. And any movie with Will Smith or Emma Stone."

"Marry me?" James asks, tucking my hair behind my ear.

"Okay." I lean closer and I slowly close my eyes. He swipes my legs off the coach, grabs my hand, and pulls me up with him.

"Let's make some lunch," he says.

∞ ∞ ∞

Another week passes, and then another. Or at least I think so, anyway. We can't get phone reception down here so it's hard to tell. The lovebirds are still on their never ending honeymoon and it's my personal opinion that they'll get married and live happily ever after if we can survive the USI.

James and I are a different story. We are definitely not lovebirds and it's starting to feel like we will never be. But the arguing between us has simmered down and we have become very close. I've never made a friend this fast before, but he could be giving Em a run for her money in the best friend department. We fit together like two puzzle pieces. We can talk about anything. It's just natural.

James decided that he had to venture up to the surface since we're running low on food. While he's gone I practice a little bit with the Gift and study my mom's journal. It's hard to teach yourself—I don't know how my mom did it. I'm getting better at invisibility, but my mom was right it's either the easiest or hardest thing for someone to learn and for me, it's the hardest.

My thoughts turn to James. I miss having someone to talk to. Well, not even talk to, but to look at. James has a boxy face with a sharp-cut jaw, thick eyebrows, rosy plump lips, and eyes that steal my soul. I could just stare at him for hours.

I hear footprints coming down the narrow stairs.

"James?" I never thought I would want him back so badly.

A small cylindrical tube bounces down the stairs and into the room. "Run!" I shout. Em and Tristen make a break up the stairs. A gray gas bursts out of the tube, filling the air.

My only option is to fight my way out. Choking from the gas, I start up the stairs, where Em and Tristen are wrestling with four men.

Interrogated

WHERE AM I? I CAN'T SEE ANYTHING. My head is ringing. I need to get out of here. I try to lift my arms, but something's holding me down. I can't feel anything but the cold cement against my back. I try to focus, but everything hurts. Somehow they must have drained my energy.

A harsh light flickers, then becomes steady. It takes my eyes a minute to adjust to the brightness. Everything's blurry. Someone's across from me, pressed against the wall.

Em? Oh, Em. What have I gotten you into? James is pressed against the wall to my left, Tristen on my right. They're all unconscious. And hanging in restraints a few feet off the ground, like we're being crucified.

The room is square, plain, and cement. One door to my right is the only way in or out.

I can barely breathe. I focus all my attention on breaking open these restraints, but there's not a drop of energy left in me.

How did the USI find us? We never left that basement.

James. He's covered in bruises. The USI must have found him. Maybe they beat our location out of him. But I think he's too strong for that. Maybe they followed him back to the basement, then grabbed him once they knew where we were. He must have fought back hard.

I want to ask if anyone's awake, but my mouth won't open. All I can do is hang and wait.

There's no way to tell time. No clock. Minutes could have passed or hours, I don't know, but James finally begins to wake up.

"Mmm," I moan, still unable to open my mouth.

James takes his time regaining consciousness. Confusion disappears and the nerves settle in—I can see it in his eyes. "Paris, I'm so sorry," he says. "This is my fault."

"Mmm," I moan again, hoping he'll understand.

"Why can't you talk?"

Why would you ask that if you know I can't talk? I try and fail to shake my head.

The door bursts open. A young man walks in, someone I have never seen before. James starts shouting questions that the intruder ignores. Instead he walks directly over to me. He reaches up and rips off the clear substance that was stretched over my mouth, then walks away, slamming the door behind him. The second that thing leaves my lips, something changes inside me. I feel pure, uncontaminated, and more alive. I open my mouth wide, taking in a large breath.

"Where are we?" I ask, maybe he knows more since he was taken years ago.

"I…" James shakes his head. "It's definitely the USI, but I don't know where. Probably a secondary base somewhere in London."

"How did we get here? I can't remember anything."

"I don't know. Paris, we need to find a way out of here. The USI tortured me for two weeks straight and I was just a little kid at the time. I'm afraid once they get everything they need from us, they might kill us." His tone is calm, but his eyes are wide and rolling in their sockets like a cornered animal's.

"We can't escape if I don't know the truth," I say. "You trust me, right? Tell me how you blocked—"

"Shhh! They're listening. Don't tell them anything. No matter what they do."

The door bursts open again. It's Terrence, followed by the same man who came in earlier.

"Well, isn't this just great? There goes the easy way. Maybe it's time we offer a little persuasion."

"We won't give you anything," James says. Both agents begin to laugh.

"Everyone cracks at some point," Terrence says with a gleaming smile. He's making me nauseous. How could someone find so much joy in the thought of hurting others?

The second agent walks over to Em and then Tristen and injects each of them with a syringe. Instantly they both spring awake. They take a couple of minutes to adjust to the situation before fear settles on their faces. The second agent walks out, leaving us with Terrence.

"So who do you want me to torture first?" Terrence asks me. "Your best friend or your big brother?" Terrence laughs at the shock and confusion on my face. "Oh you didn't know. How interesting."

"Paris, I can explain," Tristen says.

"How could you not tell me?" I ask.

"It's complicated."

"Oh, I'm sure it is." I say. Why didn't my dad tell me? How could he keep the fact that I have a brother a secret?

"As interesting as this revelation is, I'm on a bit of a tight schedule," Terrence says. "So if you don't mind—and you don't—I have a few questions for you. And if you could please answer honestly that would be splendid."

No one says a word. Terrence circles the room like a vulture stalking his prey. After three laps he stops in front of me. "Where is your mother?" he asks. I remain silent. Terrence takes a step closer. "Where is Nikki Taylor?"

"I don't know."

Terrence punches me in the face. I grunt in pain while Em screams. Terrence grabs me by my hair and slams my head into the wall. Consciousness dims, and memories begin to flood back in. The mist from the basement, it wasn't just some gas—it shocked me, electrocuted me.

"What was the mist?" I groan.

"What?" Terrence asks.

"To take me out. The mist."

"Oh, just a little something my team concocted in the lab," Terrence whispers in my ear. "It fried your brain. Just enough to destroy the Gift, but not kill you."

"I don't believe you."

"I guess you'll never know."

"What was that thing on my mouth?"

"Enough questions," Terrence says. "It's my turn. Where's Nikki Taylor?"

"Like I said, I don't know."

Terrence slams my head against the wall again. I spit on his face.

"Is that the best you got?" I mumble under my breath.

"Oh, little girl I'm just getting started."

He punches me in the gut—once, twice, again and again until I lose track. I can't breathe, and panic sets in as it feels like I'm going to suffocate.

"Stop! Stop!" James shouts. "Hit me instead!"

"I'm going to ask again," Terrence says. "Where did she go?"

"I'm telling you the truth," I gasp. "I don't know. I haven't seen my mom since I was two years old."

Terrence tilts his head, almost as if he believes me. "Okay, we'll come back to that. How does the Gift work?"

"I don't know the answer to that either."

He punches me dead in the face. A wall of blackness rolls down over my vision.

I moan as I lift my head. I try to focus, but the pain is overwhelming.

"Finally, you're awake," Terrence says.

"Leave her alone." James shouts.

I push the pain aside and stare at Terrence. He shakes his bloody hands as he walks toward me. Whose blood? I glance around the room and see that Tristen's head is hanging down with blood dripping from his face.

"How does the Gift work?" Terrence asks. "How have you received training?"

"I don't know how it works, and no, I haven't received any training."

"I don't have time for this." Terrence pulls out a gun. "You have fought off my agents several times. Clearly, you understand the Gift. Just tell me how you do it."

I glance at his gun. He wouldn't shoot me. Would he?

"Please," Terrence says. He lifts the gun and presses to my forehead.

"You can't kill her!" James shouts.

Terrence smiles at me, then slowly turns around and points the gun at James. "I could certainly kill you…"

I grind my teeth together, fighting back a scream. Terence cocks the gun.

"Stop!" I shout. "Okay, I'll tell you." Terrence lowers the gun and turns back to me. "You have to think of the Gift as a part of you. There can't be a division, because in reality the Gift and you are one."

"How do you control it?" Terrence asks.

"If you accept the Gift then it becomes natural."

"Cut the bull. I don't want the fairy princess believe in yourself crap." Terrence jams the gun against my cheek.

"You're not going to kill me," I say. "You need me."

Terrence points the gun at James again.

"You need him too." I say, taking a risky guess.

"You're right." Terrence lowers his gun, then holsters. "But I don't need her." He walks toward Em, drawing a knife as he strides across the room.

"No," Em gasps.

Terrence presses the knife against her throat. "Paris, I'm going to give you one last chance."

"You wouldn't," I say. "You wouldn't hurt an innocent defenseless person. You can't!" I argue.

Terrence just smiles. He lowers the knife from her neck and slices from her shoulder to her elbow.

Tristen yells as a trail of blood trickles down Em's fingers. Terrence slashes her forearm, and more blood spatters the concrete floor. Em, unable to flinch at the pain, closes her eyes. James, Tristen, and I are screaming.

Terrence moves on to the next arm. "If this continues, she'll bleed out," he warns. "I'll give you a minute to think about it." He walks out of the room, slamming the door shut behind him.

"Em, are you okay?" I ask.

Silence follows. Then Em slowly lifts her head to look me in the eyes and responds. "Yes."

"We're going to make it through this," Tristen says. "Stay strong."

"Don't forget—they can hear us," James says.

"What are we going to do?" Em asks. "I can't take any more of this." Tears are falling from her face and mixing with the blood beneath her feet.

"I'm going to figure something out," Tristen says. "I'm going to get us out of here."

I want to believe him, but I just can't see how. Maybe they know something I don't from the first time they escaped from this place. Maybe there's some secret. I hope.

Time passes with no way of telling how much. My stomach growls. I need food. And water.

No, what I need most is to get in touch with my mom. She would be able to get us out of here and she would know if Terrence was lying about the Gift or not. The Gift is a part of me. It's who I am now. You can't just shock that away. He must be lying. When they took whatever that thing was off my mouth, something changed inside me. It was like someone removed the dam and the water began to flow again.

The pool of blood is growing at Em's feet. My eyes are teary just looking at her. I did this to my best friend. When

I get out of here I'm going to kill Terrence and every last one of them. I'm going to make them pay.

The door bursts open and Terrence and the other agent walk back in. They unstrap Em, who falls to the ground, too weak to hold herself up.

"Your time is up," Terrence says. He starts to drag Em out of the room, tracing a thick band of blood across the floor.

"Where are you taking her?" Tristen asks.

"She's no longer of use to us."

"No," I whisper.

Terrence ignores me.

"Stop!" I shout. "I'll tell you."

Terrence drops Em in the middle of the room, steps outside, and comes back in dragging a chair. He sets it down in front of me and takes a seat.

"Well?"

"I still don't understand how this all happened," I say, "but I do know that because my mom and I were both exposed at the same time, we formed a connection."

"Paris don't," James says.

"What kind of connection?" Terrence asks.

"It's a channel that allows open communication between the two of us through dreams, impressions, ideas, and such. At least I think. Whenever I was in trouble I began having one of these dreams."

"What happened in these dreams?"

"I would see my mom teaching me how to use the Gift."

"And this happened because you were exposed at the same time?"

"That's the only explanation I can think of," I say.

"How do you control it?"

"I don't."

Terrence stands up and kicks the chair to the side of the room. He walks over to Em and grabs her by the wrists.

"I'm telling the truth!" I shout. "I don't control it. I don't know how. My mom controls it."

"Nikki, Nikki, Nikki," Terrence says. "Everything always leads back to her. Where is she?" Terrence asks.

"I don't know."

"Use your connection to find her."

"It doesn't work like that," I say.

"Do you know where she is?" Terrence asks, scanning Tristen and James. They shake their heads, glaring at him with anger bleeding through their eyes.

"Pity." Terrence starts dragging Em toward the door.

"No!" Tristen shouts. His eyes fill up with tears. "I'll tell you everything I know if you just let her go."

Terrence drops Em to the floor. "You tell me where Nikki is and I'll let her go."

"I don't know where she is exactly," Tristen says. "All she told me was she was going to the States to see Maverick. She said that he was in need and that she would be back in a couple of weeks."

"That's not good enough," Terrence says. He nods at the other agent, who takes up Em's wrists again. "I need a location."

"Okay, okay, stop. Don't hurt her. She mentioned Maine and Alpine, Utah, but that's all I know. I swear."

"Thank you for your help." Terrence looks over to the agent. "Take her."

"You promised!" I shout.

Terrence grins. "I've never been good at keeping promises." He slams the door closed on his way out.

"Emily!" Tristen shouts.

She's gone.

More time passes. No one speaks. We don't have the energy. I try to convince myself that Em is okay. They used her for leverage once, right? Why would they throw that away.

An itch starts to tickle my nose. It seems like a silly thing to worry about, but it's maddening. Anger and suppressed panic fight for dominance within me.

How did they block the Gift? Did it have something to do with those chips we saw, the ones implanted above the agents' ears? No, Terrence and the agent who dragged Em away didn't have them. Not to mention that I can't get inside Tristen's head either. They must have done something to me. What if it's permanent? I struggled to accept the Gift but now I don't think I could live without it.

"James," I say. He moans. "Do you know if Terrence was telling the truth about the Gift?"

"What do you mean?"

"Is it really gone forever? Is that possible?"

Something ripples across his face. Was that guilt? "I'm not sure," he says. "Ask Terrence."

"I don't think he's going to tell me."

The door slams open.

"How do you know who I am?" Terrence asks.

"Camden said your name when you asked him to cuff me in the woods," I say.

Terrence glares at me.

"Why do you care if I know your name?" I ask.

He doesn't answer.

"Is the Gift really gone? How did you block the Gift in London? What do you want with us? Is Em—?"

"You don't get to ask the questions here," he interrupts. "But as for the Gift, you can thank James for that." He marches out of the room and shuts the door.

James? What could he have to do with this? Is he working for Terrence like Camden? Did he give up our location? I look at him with suspicion, even though I know that's what Terrence wants.

"Paris I—"

"You what? You lied to me? No, Paris, I don't know anything about how they were able to take away the Gift. You should ask the agent," I say in a mocking tone.

"I wanted to tell you, but they were listening," James says. "I can't explain it here but I promise I'll tell you when it's safe."

"Safe?" I shout. "We are going to die in here and there's nothing you or I can do about it."

"How could you say that?" Tristen asks. "Of course we're not going to die. Someone will come."

"No one is coming because no one knows we're here!"

"Then I'll find a way out of here myself," Tristen says. "And rescue Em."

"Paris, you can't give up hope," James says.

"Hope left me," I say. "I had hope that my mom would come back after she left us. That someday my family would be reunited. That I could rescue my dad. That Camden would help me. That I would find my mom in London. Not one of those things happened. Not one."

"But they still could," James says. "You never know what's going to happen in the—"

"Just drop it," I say. "I'm done."

No one speaks after that. An hour passes—or two, or five, or ten—and I fall asleep.

Cumberland

MAVERICK STARES OUT THE WINDOW of the USI's car, regretting his choices that led him to this situation. Wishing he could be out protecting Paris. He thinks back to the moment that changed his life forever. At the time, Ryker and Rick were second and third in command at the New Mexico base. The team of Terrence, Ryker, and Rick were unstoppable, the best agents you could find.

∞   ∞   ∞

"Ryker!" I call out, desperate to share the secret that we have been chasing for years. "Ryker! I confirmed it. We have to go—now."

"How did you confirm it?" Ryker asks as he follows me out of the operations room.

"Not here."

We hurry through the dark hallways to the garage, hop in a car, and speed away.

"Well?" Ryker asks.

"It's worse than we thought. McCray's behind it all."

"I don't understand. Terrence is the best commander the USI has ever had."

I shrug. "I think what happened to his wife messed him up. And he knows about Nikki's research. I'm not sure how, but he does and I overheard his plan. He wants to steal the Gift and weaponize it."

"What? There's no way he could get away with that. We'd lose our funding."

"That's what I thought at first," I say, "but he's planning to stage an accident proving that the Gift is dangerous and argue that we need a counter weapon just as powerful."

"Rick…"

"I know. New Mexico's no longer safe. Especially with the baby on the way."

"You should check out Maine," Ryker suggests. "Lots of backcountry where no one would think to look."

"And you?"

"I'll keep an eye on Terrence."

I scowl.

"There's nothing more we can do," Ryker says. "Not until we have proof."

"Yes, but if you stay there may not be another chance to get out."

"I'm willing to take the risk. With Nikki's research you're going to need someone on the inside. Plus, I don't have a family to protect like you do."

I nod. As much as I don't want Ryker to stay, the world needs him more than me.

I pull into my driveway.

"Rick, cross reference everything we know about Terrence with the name Virgil Finnegan," Ryker says. "I overheard the name in a conversation between Terrence and his wife a while ago. It may be nothing, but just to be sure."

"Of course. I'll call you as soon as I know. Also, I'm going to resign tonight. I'll tell him that with the new baby I need a job where I don't put my life at stake. Do you think he'll buy that?"

"He's not going to waste any time deciding whether or not he believes you. But to be safe you need to disappear —tonight."

Nikki and I load the car with our emergency bags, leaving almost everything behind. We say goodbye to Ryker and hit the road. We need to put a lot of distance between New Mexico and ourselves before anyone realizes we're gone. Once Terrence finds out we've left, he's going to be terrifying.

After hours and hours of driving, we pull off the freeway and check into a motel. Nikki's too pregnant to drive, and I may get in an accident if I go any longer without sleep. I call Terence and inform him of my resignation. He argues at first but eventually says he understands. After a couple hours of sleep I begin cross-referencing Terrence McCray and Virgil Finnegan through the FBI, CIA, and other databases.

I can't believe the results. Terrence McCray's real name must be Virgil Finnegan. He was born in Alberta, Canada, to Dux and Ruby Finnegan. His father was a brilliant scientist who conducted multiple experiments attempting to increase human strength. The USI looked into his research and deemed it dangerous. They asked him to choose a new topic to study. He refused, packed up his family, and moved to Australia. After years of staying hidden, the USI tracked him down. Both he and his wife were killed defending his life studies.

Virgil, aka Terrence, was only a little boy at the time—though old enough to remember—and was placed in foster care. He jumped from foster home to foster home until he was eighteen years old and was finally able to go off on his own. He disappeared after that and no one went looking for him. He changed his name, created a new backstory, and began making his way up the ranks at the USI. He still has to answer to the panel controlling the USI but he has freedom to operate the New Mexico base as he sees fit. His performance has been outstanding—he's stopped threats from all over the world. As I stare at my laptop I decide this is all some long play to avenge his parents, and whatever his plan is, seizing the Gift is the key.

I call Ryker to deliver the information, ditch the phone, and get back on the road. Next stop Cumberland, Maine.

∞　　∞　　∞

The car comes to a sudden stop, snapping Rick out of his memories. He taps on the glass divider.

"What's going on?"

"Gas," the agent in the front says.

"Can I use the restroom while you fill up?" Rick asks.

"Wyatt, you take him."

Wyatt uncuffs Rick and shoves him toward the bathroom. "Okay," Wyatt says, handing Rick a stack of cash and a set of car keys. "It's a red Camry in the lot on the other side of this ditch."

"Thank you, I owe you big time." Rick says, going in for a hug.

"I don't need a hug—you've got to punch me. Then go and stop Terrence."

"I will. It's good to see you," Rick says as he cocks his fist.

At the End of the Tunnel Is a Train

I SLOWLY AWAKE TO THE realization that someone is messing with my ankle.

"I don't have to use the bathroom." I moan.

I look down to see the back of an agent's head as he unlocks my right leg, then my left. He doesn't have any food, so what do they want now? He stands up and frees my arms and stomach, and I crumple to the floor. I don't even have the strength to curl my fingers into a fist.

"What's going on?" James asks.

"Shhh!" the agent says. "We can't make a sound or else they'll know." What? The agent unstraps James and Tristen. "We need to hurry," he says.

"But I can't move," I say. "My legs won't hold me up."

The agent walks over and injects me with a syringe. I shoot up full of life and energy. He does the same for James and Tristen, who both rise to their feet. For the first time I notice that the agent is wearing a mask.

"Okay, put these on and follow me," he says, pulling uniforms out of his backpack and tossing them to us. "Keep your heads down and don't draw attention."

I poke the agent in the back when we step out into the hallway. "I'm not leaving without Em," I say.

"We don't have a choice," he says. There's something familiar in his voice. "We'd be caught, and you'd lose your only chance of getting out of here."

"We could—"

"No, the only option is to get you out of here so that we can get reinforcements and come back for her."

"But what if we—"

"No. It's the only way," he says. He grabs my arm and pulls me down the hallway. I hesitate at first, pushing back against his grip. But he's right—this is the only way. I'll come back for you Em, I promise.

The agent presses a button at the end of the hallway. An enormous black door sinks into the floor, revealing a featureless desert that stretches out to the horizon.

"Where are we?" I ask.

A loud siren goes off.

"Follow me," the agent says. He turns right and starts to sprint, his shoulder just an inch from the building's wall. Running it is.

We follow the side of the building and turn a corner. The agent swipes his badge and pulls open a side door, leading us into a giant garage. There has to be more than fifty identical black cars lined up side by side in a never ending line.

"These two," the agent says, pointing to the first two in the row. I slide into the driver's seat of the first car while the agent takes the wheel of the second.

"Paris, be careful. I hope it doesn't come to this, but I loaded the back seats with a couple guns just in case."

James climbs into the passenger seat of my car while Tristen gets in with the agent. As soon as the garage door is halfway open, the agent speeds off. I start the car and slam down on the gas, the unexpected acceleration shoving me back into my seat.

"Why do I have a feeling that a high-speed car chase is about to take place?" I ask.

"Because if it didn't then our life would just be too easy," James says.

"Are we clear so far?"

"I don't see anybody, but that alarm wasn't calling them to dinner."

"Where are we going, anyways? All I see is desert."

"Who knows? Just follow the other car." James glances over his shoulder. "Oh crap. Paris, step on it!"

"I'm already going as fast as I can. How many?"

"I don't know! Maybe twenty, I can't tell. They're gaining on us though."

I continue to follow the agent's car as it swerves between the sand dunes. His tires are kicking up so much sand that I can barely see.

"James, I'm going to crash. What do I do?"

"Go left," he says. "Get clear of this mess."

I veer left and speed out of the cloud of sand. After a few minutes of swerving between sand dunes like they're black diamond moguls I lose the agents completely. How are we ever going to find Tristen again?

A loud thump makes me jump in my seat. "What was that?" I ask.

"A gunshot, I think," James says. "The rear window's chipped."

"How many?"

"It's hard to see in all this dust, but I see two cars right behind us."

More shots fire, over and over.

"Good thing the car's bulletproof," James says.

"Could you stop looking on the bright side and do something?" I snap.

"Like what?"

"Grab that gun in the back seat and shoot back."

"Pretty sure their cars are bulletproof too," he says.

"Then shoot the tires!"

James rolls down the window and opens fire. I glance in the rearview window to see the front-left tire of the lead car explode. The car lifts into the air, then lands on its side before it's sent tumbling across the sand as the next two cars slam into it.

"Nice shot," I shout.

"Paris, I've been on the run my entire life. What do you think I did in my free time? Puzzles? Arts and crafts? Of course I'm a good shot."

"Stop bragging and keep shooting!"

"They've fallen back," James says. "We might actually get out of this after all."

We hit a flat stretch with no dunes and I gunned the accelerator. "Are they still chasing us?" I shout.

"I can't see through all this dust. And be careful, okay? We don't know what's ahead of us."

"I'm always careful," I say with a laugh. I have to say that I'm loving driving this car. It's awesome and I think I'm pretty good at it.

My laughter fades when I see a line of black dots on the horizon. I whip the wheel to the right but they're approaching from that direction. It's the USI, and we're surrounded. At least ten cars in front of us and who knows how many chasing us from behind.

"What do we do?" I ask.

"Stop," James says. "Stay in the car."

I ease off the gas and slow to a stop. James opens his car door and flings his rifle into the sand. He starts to get out and I grab his arm.

"No!" I shout. "Let me go."

"Paris, you don't have the Gift right now. They'll just kill you."

"But they'll kill you if you go."

James smirks. "I thought you didn't like me."

"Why would you say that?"

"All the arguing before we were captured."

"Are you kidding? That was all you. Look, I already lost Em and my parents, and now Tristen's gone, who knows if they made it out. I can't lose you too."

"I didn't know I meant that much to you."

"I didn't say that—"

James cut me off with a kiss. Only a couple of seconds, but the best couple of seconds I've had in months. My heart turns heavy and melts through my chest.

"Okay," I say, pulling on his arm. "Now there's no way I'm letting you get out of this car."

"Everything will be okay." He twists free and steps out onto the desert with his hands above his head.

"Please," I beg as he walks toward the agents.

"You stupid boy, it's the girl we want," an agent says.

"Well she's not in there, she got into the other car." James says.

Two agents pull out a rocket launcher and point it at my windshield.

"What are you doing?" James shouts.

"Our orders are to bring you in dead or alive," says the agent holding the RPG, "and personally I find dead more fun." He fires off the rocket and I dive out of the car as the concussion from the blast ripples through me.

"Looks like someone's a little liar," an agent says. "Get her."

Agents charge toward me, grab my arms, and start wrestling me back to the group.

"Paris!" James shouts. "Use the Gift! You can do it!"

I focus all of my remaining energy on the Gift but it doesn't work. Nothing's working. I don't even feel smart anymore. "It's gone!" I shout back.

The two agents throw me into the back seat of a car and cuff me to the grab handle. The other agents slide into their cars and the caravan begins its way back to the base.

"Why do you work for the USI?" I ask. "All they do is hurt innocent people."

"Shut up," one agent answers.

"No seriously, why?"

"We save lives." the other says.

"Is that what you think? You think you're the heroes?" I try to contain my laughter. Neither agent responds. "Wow, did my beauty render you guys speechless? Or was it my black eye?" Silence again. "That's what I thought."

Concussions shake the windows as the two cars flanking us explode into the air. I glance through the back window just in time to see another car. And another. I search desperately for the source, then I see something flying straight for us. Holy—

The next thing I know we're upside down and tumbling through the sand. Gravity jerks me to the ceiling with a sharp wrench of my shackled wrist. When the car settles to a stop I realize that I'm covered in blood.

Someone yanks open the car door and tries to pull me out by my waist. "Hands cuffed," was all I managed to get out.

∞   ∞   ∞

Where am I? Ow, my head.

I feel a hand running through my hair. James? I lift my head off of his lap, full of confusion.

"Paris, you're okay. Don't move."

I ignore him and sit up. I glance around the car. James, Tristen, and the masked agent—we all made it.

"How long have I been out? What happened?"

"You can thank these two," James said. "Or blame our masked friend for not giving us an RPG. Tristen sniped the agents holding me and Zorro here went all shock and awe on their cars. Then we chased down the escort. We weren't sure which car you were in, so we just shot them all. Sorry."

James pauses, searching for forgiveness in my eyes. I punch him in the arm, although I think it hurts my burned hand more than him.

"What was that for?" he asks.

"That was for shooting me with a rocket launcher." I lean in and kiss him on the cheek. "And that's for rescuing me."

James blushes. "Right. Sorry about the rocket, but it's good to see you again."

"So where are we?" I ask. I look out the windows and see a thick forest of pine trees lining both sides of a one-lane dirt road. "How long have I been out?"

"Colorado," the agent says. "Rio Grande National Forest. We'll hike up into the mountains and rest for a few days."

An hour later he pulls the car off the road and opens the trunk. "We've got tents, food, and water purifiers—"

"Enough," I say. "I'm not going to hike into the mountains with some masked maniac who shot me with an RPG. Who are you?"

The agent sighs, then pulls off his mask.

CHAPTER 14

A Mother Knows

"RICK?"

"Hi, sweetie. There's been an emergency. I need you to come as soon as you can."

"What kind of emergency?" Nikki asks.

"The USI. Paris managed to get away with her friends but I couldn't. I escaped from USI custody with Wyatt and Jack's help a couple of weeks ago but I haven't been able to find her."

"I'm glad you're safe. I've actually been sending her visions. Any day now José should be sending her to London. I planned to be here when she arrived, but the weirdest thing happened."

"What?"

"Ryker called me."

"Ryker?" Rick asks.

"The one and only. I have no clue how he got my number."

"What did he want?"

"He wants me to come to the States. He said more memories have surfaced and he has crucial information about Terrance's plan."

"And you trust him."

"You don't?" Nikki asks.

"He's my brother—I want nothing more than to trust him, but the Ryker I know is gone."

"I think you're wrong. He's changed. I told him to go find Paris."

"You did what?"

"She was in danger! I got a tip from Jack and Wyatt that the USI had locked on to her location. Ryker saved her life."

Rick lowers the phone and closes his eyes. "Okay," he says after a moment. "Tell him to come to the safe house in Arizona. I'll be here waiting."

"Sounds good. I'll be there tomorrow."

Nikki disconnects the phone and dissembles it, breaking the circuit board into pieces and flushing them one by one. Moving quietly to keep from waking Tristen and James, she packs a bag for her flight. It hurts that she has to go—Paris is going to arrive any day now, and she deserves some answers—but this is a life of constant sacrifice.

Public transportation is out of the question—too many cameras, so she takes a cab to Heathrow. When the taxi stops at a red light she makes herself invisible and erases herself from the driver's mind. He stops at the taxi stand by the arrivals zone for Terminal 4, and she waits for him to reach the front of the line. Then she slips out when he opens the door for his next passenger and begins the long walk toward the departures wing of the terminal.

The first direct flight to Phoenix would leave at 12:25. At Nikki's direction, the attendant refuses to let an irate first-class passenger board. Settling into the empty seat, she closes her eyes and finally gets some sleep.

"Ladies and gentlemen, this is your captain speaking, we are beginning our descent into the Phoenix airport. It is 3:04 in the afternoon and as sunny as always. Thank you for flying British Airways and enjoy your day."

Nikki is a little startled when she wakes up. She's never slept through an entire flight before. As the other passengers disembark, she attempts to plan out exactly what she would say to Rick and Ryker. What do you say to your husband whom you only get to see once a year? Or his brother, who was an ally, then brainwashed, and has now turned back onto your side? No words describe her emotions, and no emotions fit the situation. She'll just have to wing it.

Nikki slips into another passenger's taxi, and after the man is dropped off at his home in suburban Mesa, she waits on his doorstep for a few minutes and then rings the doorbell. When he answers the door she convinces him to sell her his car for a euro, making a mental note to pay him back later. It's a crappy thing to do, but it's hard not to do crappy things when you're in a situation like this. It's either cheat or quit.

After three hours of driving Nikki arrives at the cabin. She stands at the front door and tries to compose herself. If Ryker's information is as important as he says it is, it could change the course of their war. She enters the house code and steps inside.

"Nikki!" Rick picks her up in a hug so tight that she can barely breathe. Then he gently sets her down and kisses her ever so perfectly. Their love is infinite—fighting all time and space.

Ryker knocks on the door just ten minutes later, cutting their reunion short. He gathers Nikki and Rick in a big group hug.

"I don't mean to jump straight to this," Nikki says, "but what's so important that you can't tell me over the phone?"

Ryker smiles. "Can't a weary traveler sit down and have a can of Diet Dr. Pepper?"

"Well I'm the one who's been in transit for eighteen hours, and I was invisible for most of that, so—"

"Guys, guys," Rick interrupts. "Come to the kitchen and I'll get you both some."

"I wasn't sure how long it would take to get my memories back," Ryker said as they sat down. "All I knew was those were my memories and I wanted them now. I decided to break into the New Mexico base and broke into Terrence's office. I found a ton of information about you living in London. They've had spies on you for weeks, tracking every single move you make. That's why I couldn't tell you what I knew. I had to get you out of there without compromising our advantage."

"They know about London?" Nikki shouts. "I left James and Tristen there, and Paris is on her way!"

"I'm so sorry, Nikki, but there was no alternative."

"I'm going to call them," Nikki says.

"If you do that, they'll be in USI custody before they're out the door," Ryker says. "They're using them as bait, just like they were using you. Paris is all they care about now."

"Was that everything?" Rick asks.

"That's just the tip of the iceberg. I found enough to take down the USI—if we play our hand just right. If not... well..."

CHAPTER 15

A Love Betrayed

"STAY AWAY FROM ME!" I shout.

"What's going on? Who is he?"

"Leave! Get away!" I shout. He simply stares at me with a steady, expressionless face. He must have learned that in USI training.

"Paris, you don't understand."

"I don't want to understand. I don't care. James, Tristen, we're leaving!"

"Paris, calm down," Tristen says. "What's going on?"

"We can't trust him," I say. "This is a trap. We need to leave right now!"

"Paris, he saved your life…" James says, touching my arm. I shake him off.

"Par, please." Camden whispers.

I slap him in the face. "You don't get to call me that. I don't ever want to see you again."

"Just let me explain—"

"I've heard enough of your lies!"

"This is the truth, Paris," Camden says.

"It's never the truth!"

"Just give him a chance," Tristen says. "He saved our lives."

Camden closes his eyes. "When I was eleven my brother and I were finally placed with a really awesome family—or at least they seemed awesome. They worked for the USI. When I started to act out they took my little brother away. He was only three years old. They began to teach me how to fight, to shoot, to code … I didn't want any of it. If I was good they let me see him twice a year. Twice a year. On his birthday, and on my birthday. Then they told me that I was going to move to Utah, to meet you. That I would go on my first mission. I refused. That's when they threatened to kill him. They threatened to kill a little nine-year-old boy."

Camden looks up at me with sorrow. Unsure of what to do, I flick the fingers of my crossed right arm, gesturing for him to continue.

"They forced me to get involved in your life, to watch you, and notify them when the Gift activated. They would send me videos of Jackson being held in cells with no sunlight, eating gruel with maggots in it. Terrence use to say that the more intel I gave him the better life Jackson would have.

"I did whatever they asked. I had to—he's my brother. But I swear to you, all my feelings for you were real. It was my mission to get close to you. It wasn't my mission to date you. Once I met you I fell in love. Paris, I love you."

Now it's my turn to close my eyes. I'm still angry, but it's that frustrated sort of anger that you're not quite sure you should be holding onto.

"Camden, I'm sorry for what happened to your parents. I'm sorry for Jackson…that's…terrible. And maybe at some point in the past I loved you too, but then you broke my heart. You were the one person I thought I could trust unconditionally. That's gone, and it's gone forever."

I can't see his expression—tears have blurred my vision.

"I do believe that what you're telling me is true. I do believe that you're a good person. You can stay, but don't tell me that you love me anymore, okay? What we had is dead."

"I…I'm so sorry," Camden says. "I tried to tell them as little as possible but I had to protect my brother."

"He's your brother, yes, but I'm a person too. And so is Em. You were willing to condemn the two of us to torture and murder to save one life. And you weren't even saving him! He's no better off now than he was when you betrayed us. And how many more people will you hurt until you realize that they're never going to set him free?"

"Paris," James says. "Easy. The kid's nine years old."

Camden looks at me with his bright blue eyes. "I'll do everything I can to regain your trust. I promise."

My gut is telling me to believe him. The dream proves it, anyway. I just wish he had come clean while we were still dating.

"I can't think about this anymore." I step past Camden and grab one of the backpacks out of the trunk. "We need to set up camp before it's dark. James, Tristen, you can come clean along the way. Stop giving me puzzle pieces and just give me the full picture."

"Of course," Tristen says.

We start up the slope with Camden leading the way. He walks about ten steps ahead of us, close enough to hear but remaining outside of our group. His posture slopes to the left under the weight of the heavy duffle bag full of weapons he's carrying.

"You're my brother?"

Tristen nods. "I didn't know when or how to tell you."

"Well, now's your chance."

"I was five years old when you and Mom contracted the Gift."

"But I don't remember you."

"And I don't remember you. I didn't live at home. I had autism. A very severe form of it, and I was a danger to myself."

"But you, um…"

Tristen smiles. "Seem fine now? Mom found a way to heal me with the Gift when I was seven. Pretty impressive, really, since ever since her friend got me out of my institution the two of us were always on the run. I'm sorry we never reached out, but it wasn't safe."

"But you knew about me—why didn't Dad tell me?"

"You can't blame them for this. They were both making difficult choices."

"Well," I say after a moment, "I'm glad I have an older brother."

Tristen punches my shoulder. "And I'm glad I have you. We have a lot of catching up to do."

We walk on in silence.

"And what's your story," I ask James.

"I don't know where to start."

"Why don't you give it your best shot?"

"Well, I was also given the Gift but apparently it affected me differently. My brain started to act almost like a shield. When the USI kidnapped us the first time they ran tests on me, trying to find ways to replicate what I can do. They extracted a lot of bone marrow, as well as something from my brain. After a couple weeks of testing we escaped and I wasn't sure how much they learned until we saw them in London. I think those chips on the side of their head blocked you from getting inside their head. I thought that was all they knew how to do, but I guess I was wrong. Somehow they found a way to block your Gift altogether. I don't know if it's permanent or temporary."

"Well, we need to find out. I need the Gift if we're going to rescue Em."

"I don't know about what they did to you," Camden says without turning around, "but maybe it's temporary. Those chips only last for twenty-four hours."

"And what else do you know?" I ask.

"There isn't much to tell. Terrence didn't trust me. I got my orders and that was it."

We set up camp in a clearing about two-thirds of the way up the mountain. Or the boys do, actually, while I sit half-slumped over our electric stove, still in pain and completely exhausted from the whirlwind of the past 24 hours. My body has never experienced such blunt force and trauma, well that is if you don't count the onset of the Gift, which apparently I don't even have anymore. When they're done James puts a blanket over my shoulders and sits down next to me. He tries to put his arm around me but I slide away. All I want to do is lie in his arms and gently kiss him, but I can't with Camden standing right there.

He said he loved me. I don't know how I feel. I don't think I love him anymore, but what if my emotions are just clouded by anger? And what about James? He's one of the best friends I've ever had. A best friend that I can't stop thinking about. I get butterflies just being close to him. Ugh, why does life have to be this complicated?

I stand up, brushing off my filthy jeans. "I'm going to gather some firewood."

"No need," Camden says. "We have the stove, and these sleeping bags are rated—"

"I'll come with you," James says. I nod. It's probably good that we talk in private.

"You load me up, and I'll carry," James said. "Sound good?"

"Sure."

We stroll into the woods, the sharp sting of pine sap prickling my nose.

"I've always wanted a home in a place like this," James says. "Secluded, beautiful, and private."

"Seems like you've had plenty of that already," I say.

He smiles. "The seclusion, sure. I've gotten used to that. But living underground like a rat..."

Not knowing what to say, I pick up a few branches of deadwood and drop them in his arms.

"I've always wanted to live on a lake," he continues. "Somewhere high up in the mountains like this. Waking up every day to peace and quiet, a place that's personal and beautiful. That's the dream." He looks up at me, smiling. Ah, every time my heart melts. His pure, caring, beautiful smile is too much to handle.

"So what's the deal between you and Camden?" he asks.

Wow, okay. I guess we'll just jump right into it then.

"Well, we dated for about a year, and honestly I thought he was the one. You heard the rest. He was working for the USI the whole time."

"Are you going to go back to him?"

"I don't know what I want anymore." I say, turning my focus from the ground to deep into his murky brown eyes. "I spent a while getting over Camden, trying to move on, and then I met you. Everything happened so quickly, but I feel like we've known each other our entire lives. Those three weeks with you were amazing. And then, well, you know what happened in the car."

"I couldn't forget even if I wanted to."

"What does that mean? You like me? I really need to know the truth. I don't think I could handle being strung along right now."

"Paris, you are the most beautiful girl I have ever seen in my life, inside and out. I want you to choose me. I want to be with you."

"James…"

"Like you said, it feels like we've known each other our entire lives. Take a risk, see where it takes you."

"James, I don't even know your last name. Don't get me wrong, I like you a lot, but don't you think we should just slow down a little?"

"Braden."

"What?"

"It's Braden. I think. And I don't think we should slow down. I feel something for you, isn't that enough? Or do you not feel the same—"

I stretch onto the tip of my toes and gently grab the back of his neck, pulling him in until our lips graze each other's. He drops the firewood and I feel his hand on my waist pulling me into him closer than I thought possible.

"Is that a yes?" James asks.

"No," I say. No? The word just jumped out of my mouth. His face drops, his smile gone.

"I mean, I don't know yet. I have so much I need to sort out right now, and my life is too crazy. I don't want to ruin what we have."

I want to say yes—why can't I get myself to say yes? I reach for James's hand, desperate for another second of warmth, but he pulls away from me.

"Whatever, I understand," he says as he turns and walks off back toward the campsite.

"I'm so sorry," I whisper, but he's too far away. "James, wait!" No response. I sigh, then bend down to pick up the firewood he dropped. The sap is sticky against my hands, and splinters jab my skin.

I drag my feet back to the campsite, in no hurry to see anyone. I need to figure out what we're going to do next. Finding my mom would be nice, though I don't have any idea how I can do that. London was our one chance.

Ow! I drop the firewood as I walk face-first into a tree branch.

Tristen laughs. "Did you zone out a little bit?"

"Something like that," I say. "You want to help me with this?"

"Sure."

As we pick up the firewood I see that James and Camden are deep in conversation in the clearing. Crap, what could they possibly be talking about?

I walk over to them, dropping the firewood at their feet. "So what's up?"

"Nothing," Camden says.

"Just talking about life," James adds.

"Okay, you don't have to tell me if you don't want." I retreat to the other side of the clearing and join Tristen for some brother-sister bonding time.

Camden makes us a dinner of canned beans and a stew made from dehydrated chicken then calls Tristen and I over. We sit down and eat by the fire, our first meal since we escaped. I didn't know food could taste this good. Camden and James aren't talking much, although I think that's Tristen and my fault. We still have so much to catch up on, endless details of our lives that need to be shared. It's different now that we know we're siblings—we can tell the same story that we told in the rabbit hole and it means something more to us now. Well, to me, that is, since Tristen already knew I was his sister.

After dinner we all continue to sit around recovering from the many traumas we endured today. Not going to lie, my head's still ringing from the explosion, and my face and ribs ache from Terrence's punches. Most of all, my emotions are a mess. Camden's return, James... Em. I try to convince myself that they aren't torturing her now that we've escaped.

Camden taps me on the shoulder. "It's getting pretty late. Maybe we should head to bed."

I yawn. "I don't think I can sleep yet. I'm going to stare at the stars for a bit."

"Mind if I stay up with you?"

"Mmm. Camden, how did we get here? How did we get to Colorado from London?"

"Military cargo plane. The USI's got an airbase not too far outside London. You were back in New Mexico when I found you."

"How long were we in there for?"

"I'm not sure exactly. About two weeks."

"What? Are you serious?"

We fall silent and watch the stars.

"Look," Camden says. "A satellite."

"How can you tell?"

"It's moving. See?"

I yawn again. "Okay, I'm going to bed." I climb into the tent I'm sharing with Tristen. Within seconds of crawling into my sleeping bag I'm out cold for the night.

Three days pass of pure rest and recovery. I'm beginning to feel guilty just lying around all day. I should be training, getting ready to fight, making a plan to rescue Em. Although I need the rest to rebuild my strength. Worryingly, there's no sign that the Gift has come back.

James and I take a stroll every morning and evening. It's the only time I leave the campsite. We clear our heads and just talk like we used to.

The sun is low in the western sky and shining a golden light on the pines in the valley below when James calls to me.

"Paris, you ready?" he asks.

"Yeah, just a second." I'm in the tent, looking for my flashlight just in case we get lost. I feel two arms gently wrap around my waist from behind. I could just stay like this forever.

"Can we talk?" Camden whispers in my ear.

I whirl around. "Um, yeah, I guess so. What is it?"

"Not here." He reaches out his hand, but I pull away. I follow him out of the tent and into the woods. I follow behind silently. After walking for a couple of minutes Camden stops abruptly and turns to face me. "What's going on with you and James?"

"I don't think that's any of your business."

"Paris, please, I still love you, I just want to know what's going on."

"He was there for me when you weren't."

"So you guys are…friends?" Camden asks.

"I don't know what we are."

"Have you kissed him?"

"That is none of your business."

"So that's a yes. You're so different now, Par. Not opening up, kissing boys you just met. It took you five months to kiss me and what, two weeks, to kiss him, a stranger."

"I've known him longer than two weeks. And you're right —I'm a different Paris than before because I've been to hell and back. I've been chased, attacked, shot, abandoned, kidnapped, tortured. I don't know if I'll ever see Em again. I don't even know if she's alive. And the only tool I had to save her is gone now too. I'm useless. So you know what? Yes, I'm different, thanks to you and your buddies at the USI."

Camden's voice drops to a whisper. "Let me help you. Let me be a part of your life again."

My eyes tear up. "How? There's nothing you can do."

"Let me teach you how to fight."

I wrap my arms around his neck, pulling him in. I've missed Camden's hugs—they're so comforting, as if nothing can happen to me. My lips brush against his ear as I whisper a thank you.

"Wait your leg! I completely forgot to ask. How is it?"

"It's great. The USI has all sorts of drugs that accelerate the healing process. It's a little stiff when it rains, but besides that and the scar I wouldn't even know that I've been shot."

"You got any more of that medication?"

"I wish. I injected the last three I had into you guys in your cell."

We walk back to the campsite, and for the first time it feels like it did before. Easy conversation, laughing. Hope begins to wave—she's back again.

Day after day passes of grueling training. Since I can no longer rely on the Gift I have to learn how to defend myself in other ways. I guess all the days spent at karate class and the shooting range with my dad really did pay off because both James and Camden say that I'm a natural. James has been teaching me everything I need to know about shooting and he's an incredible marksman. Camden is my sparring partner, teaching me hand-to-hand combat. Which I think annoys James a little because he wants to teach me everything. Tristen joins in from time to time but his skills are far beyond mine.

In my free time I do everything I can think of to rediscover the Gift, but I'm beginning to think it's gone for good. I'm trying to keep a positive attitude about it, and I'm not going to give up.

James and Camden keep fighting for my attention. I guess that means they've gotten over some of the harsher things I said. I know I can't lead both of them on forever, but another week or two of this couldn't hurt. Plus I still don't know who to choose, I feel like the decision needs to be obvious and neither is the obvious choice.

Paris Freeman, Paris Braden…Braden is sounding a little better, but I guess all I can do is let it work itself out.

This morning I woke up extra early to practice on my own. I stroll down to the range that James set up in the woods. I'm still a little wild with a handgun, but I don't miss a single shot with the rifle. Maybe I can do this without the Gift after all. I sling the rifle over my shoulder and walk farther down the trail, overwhelmed with confidence in myself. I know I should go back but the beauty of this place is mesmerizing. The other mountains in the distance, the birdsong, the regal grandeur of the trees. The sun's peeking through the canopy, creating a spotlight just on me.

A barely audible scream off in the distance steals my attention. What was that?

I run toward the scream, fending off the branches as they try to slap me in the face. I hear the scream again— I'm closer now; it's from a little girl. The next scream is so loud it's as if I'm holding her in my arms yet there's no sign of anyone. Then utter silence. I lift my hands, which are covered in gashes. Blood drops rise from the wounds and echo as they strike the ground.

"Hello? Is anyone here?" I call out into the wall of greenness that surrounds me.

"Paris!"

I look up and see a little girl clinging to a tree branch twenty feet above my head. Her blond hair blowing in the wind, white dress shimmering in the sunlight. Her innocence shining as bright as the stars. Who is this little girl? She seems so familiar.

"Paris, run! Run, and don't look back! Run straight for me! Run straight for…"

"Run where? Why?" I yell.

"Run!"

My eyes open as I dart up out of bed.

"Paris, are you okay?" Tristen asks.

"Yes, sorry. Bad dream."

"Want to talk about it?"

I shake my head. "I'm just going to get a little fresh air," I say as I crawl out of the tent. I gather my weapons and head to the shooting range. I'm still a little wild with a handgun, but I don't miss a single shot with the rifle. I continue down the trail, listening for another scream. Just as I'm about to turn back with no luck, there it is. The same voice as before. I chase it straight to the same tree, and the same little girl is hugging the branch twenty feet above me.

"What's your name?" I call up to her.

"Paris! Paris, run! Run, and don't look back! Run straight for me! Run straight for your—"

My eyes open as I dart up in bed. What is going on? Tristen asks me what's wrong but I ignore him and climb out of the tent, heading straight for the little girl. This time I walk past the range and don't wait for the scream. I just run toward her. I run through the jagged branches that are desperately trying to stop me.

Once I get to the tree I look up and see the same little girl again. "What's going on?"

"Paris! Paris, run! Run, and don't look back! Run straight for me! Run straight for your fav—"

My eyes open and I dart up out of bed. Over and over again until finally on the seventh time, it's different. On the seventh time I disappear from the woods into a darkness where I wait until the sun comes up. I crawl out of the tent to see James boiling water for our breakfast of reconstituted powdered eggs.

"What day is it?" I ask.

"Good morning to you too."

"Sorry, good morning."

"It's Friday."

So we've been here for seven days, the same as I thought when I went to bed before the little girl. That was one complicated dream. Seven layers deep into the dream —was that a coincidence? I guess it doesn't really matter because now I have the finished message. I finally know where to run to. Run straight for your favorite place on earth, was the little girl's message. I know where to go, and I know who told me. The little girl was me. This kind of confusing crap only happens through the Gift. Could that mean that it's slowly coming back?

"Camden, Tristen, wake up!" I shout.

"What's the rush?" James asks.

"I know where to go."

"You do?"

"Yes, and we're leaving in an hour."

"May I ask why?"

"A little girl reminded me."

James looks at me, then shrugs. "Alrighty."

Camden and Tristen emerge from their tents. "Ugh, the USI probably heard you shouting all the way from New Mexico," Tristen complains.

"Eat your eggs, and then let's get to packing," I say. "We're leaving in an hour."

"Where to?" Tristen asks.

"Blackfoot, Arizona."

"That's by the Hualapai Reservation?" Camden asks.

I nod.

"How do you know that?" James asks.

Camden shrugs. "Always had a thing for maps, atlases, dictionaries...The USI didn't let me out much, you know?"

James is a thoughtful cook—with the wild greens and mushrooms he foraged, he can make even powdered eggs taste good. When we're done I scour our plates and utensils with dirt and a wire brush while the others strike our tents.

"Looks like we're ready to go," Camden says. Besides the charred wood in our fire pit, there's no visible trace that we were ever here.

We hike down the mountain and begin our ten-hour drive to Blackfoot. I take the first shift with James in the front seat. I've always loved long car rides, singing our hearts out to music, playing games, deep conversations, and fun stories. This car drive is as great as always—we sing, get to know each other better, and play the alphabet game (I win), and time flies by.

The only negative is I wish we had more time. Now that we only have a half-hour to go I'm getting nervous. Who's going to be waiting for us? My mom? Or dad? The USI? We just have to wait and see.

Camden pulls off Route 66 and onto the back roads. I can see it in my mind, my favorite place in the world. A small cabin in the arid mountains, the middle of nowhere. It wasn't actually my favorite place in the world, but my dad always called it that and told me to come here if I was ever lost or in trouble. I've never actually been here, but I've seen pictures.

We're here. Camden drives off the road and stops the car a safe distance away. I can do this. I unbuckle my seatbelt, open the car door, and start walking toward the ridgeline.

CHAPTER 16

The Bond

"PARIS!"

"Dad?" My walk toward the cabin turns into a run. "Dad is that you?"

"Yes! I'm here!"

I sprint right into his arms.

"Dad! I can't believe you're here! I've missed you so much!" I break down in tears, soaking his shirt in drops of joy.

"Paris, I love you. You are so strong and brave, I'm so proud of you." I never want to let go. For a brief second I'm home, sitting in the kitchen eating our takeout leftovers for breakfast—happy, safe, loved.

He takes a step back and stares at my bruised face. "What happened to you?"

"The USI captured us, but we're okay now."

"Did, did Terrence do this to you?"

"Dad, it's in the past and I'm getting better every day."

"I'm so happy you're okay." He gives me another hug.

"Paris?"

I let go of my dad to see a woman standing a few feet away. She looks nervous, like I'm a dog that might bite.

"Mom?" I ask.

She nods, her eyes brightening with tears.

"Mom!" I rush to her and give her a hug. I may know more about my Spanish teacher than her, but she's still my mom.

"Paris, I've missed you so much," she sobs. "You have no idea just how much I love you."

"Hi, Mom," I manage to squeeze out through her hug. "I've missed you too."

"How did you escape?"

"Camden got us out."

"Camden, thank you," my dad says. He lets go of Tristen and embraces Camden.

"Mom, this is Camden," I say.

"Paris, where's Emily?" my dad asks.

"Sir, the USI still has her," Camden says.

"We have to go back for her," I say. "Now."

"Par, it's not safe yet," Camden says. "You've got to get the Gift back first."

"You mean you've lost the Gift?" my mom asks. "That's not possible."

"We all have a lot to talk about," I say. "Mom and Dad, you need to explain everything with no more secrets or lies, and Camden has some new information. So maybe we should go inside because I have a feeling this is going to take a long time."

"Of course. It's time we tell you everything." my mom agrees and we all follow her inside.

As we sit down at the kitchen table, Camden looks over at me, nervous and out of place. I have my dad, James and Tristen have my mom, but Camden has no one. "Do you want me to leave while you all talk?" he asks me.

"No, stay." I say. "We trust you."

"I guess I'll start," my mom says. "Paris, when your Gift activated, I started sending you the dreams you've been having."

"Yeah, we sort of suspected that," I say. "Because we both got the Gift at the same time, right?"

She smiles. "You're a smart young woman. I can communicate that with you, but no one else, even if they have the Gift. And you can do the same with me—in fact you have before."

"I have?"

"Several times actually, all of which were just random thoughts."

"Oh, okay." I say ignoring her vagueness. "But why did you send us to Pole Hill? We did nothing there except waste time and almost get captured. At least when you sent us to Mexico Mr. Jalisco helped us."

"It was a mistake. Sending you a memory is one thing, even if it's a memory of my own. Sending a brand-new message is harder. I don't know if you read it wrong, or if I sent it wrong, but Pole Hill was compromised many years ago."

"Why didn't I have the Gift the second I was exposed?" I ask. "Why did it 'resonate' when I turned eighteen?"

"At that stage the Gift was only for people whose brains had completely developed. Honestly, the Gift should have killed you."

"Then why didn't it?"

"I have a theory," my mom says, "but I don't think we'll ever know the real reason."

"Well, what's your theory?"

"I think it might have killed you for a short second, and your energy latched on to mine, drawing strength from me, which might have created the bond. And once the bond closed, the energy became unstable. Every time we came in contact the unstable energy would send shocks through our bodies. The worst pain I had ever felt."

"So you're saying you had to leave to help stabilize the energy and you couldn't return until the bond reopened."

"Exactly."

"How did you know when the bond would reopen?" I ask.

"I didn't know for sure. I hoped that it would be when your mind became fully developed and could handle the full potential of the Gift." She pauses. "Well, I hoped at first. After years of practicing with the Gift I had a glimpse into the future where I saw the bond reopened."

"When can I learn that?"

"It's more challenging than it sounds. I've only been successful twice and both were by accident."

"And you told Dad?"

"She did," he says, "but the USI attacked before I could begin your training."

That doesn't make sense to me—I had the Gift for several days before the USI arrived, but I squeeze my dad's hand and smile.

"How come you weren't there when I turned eighteen?" I ask.

"I wanted to be," my mom says, "but it was too dangerous. Besides, you had to connect with the Gift on your own. And you did just that. You have become strong, independent, courageous, and skilled. You trained yourself, mastered techniques by yourself. You are so talented, I'm so proud of you."

"Yeah, but the Gift's gone. Terrence said he shocked my brain and destroyed it. I didn't believe him at first but it's been weeks and the Gift isn't back yet."

"Paris, you can't shock the Gift out of someone. It's a part of you forever."

"That's what I thought at first too, but—"

"But you don't think it's back yet? Paris, I don't think the Gift was ever gone. I think you're blocking out the Gift because of the trauma you endured. If you let it back in, I'm sure that we can overcome this."

"Really?"

"Of course, sweetie," she says. "We just have to practice and figure out where the energy is being blocked. Every single living little thing has energy," she recites. I have a feeling that she's given this speech to her students many times before. "Grass, trees, plants, water, animals, humans, everything. Anyone can recognize this and tap into the energy, feeling emotions from others and helping to know what the body or thing needs. With the Gift, however, we can do more. We can draw strength from the energy sources or we can give energy. For instance, if I'm in a battle and am losing strength, anyone with the Gift could give me more energy through physical touch. But you and I can give each other energy at all times and in all places through our bond."

She looks around the room. "More than anything, this is the one secret that we need to keep from the USI."

My cheeks turn bright red and I stare down at the wooden grain of the kitchen table. I ruined everything.

"Paris, what is it?" my dad asks.

"When we were being interrogated," James says, "they threatened to kill Emily. Instead of hurting us they, they—"

"They're monsters," Tristen says.

"I'm sorry, Mom," I say. "I told them everything I knew about the bond, I just couldn't watch him torture Em."

"So they know about the bond, whatever," my mom says. "We can make that work. The most important thing is that you're here."

I breathe deeply, fighting back tears.

"Maybe we should take a break?" my mom asks. "Go for a walk and clear our heads?"

"No, I'm okay. I have so many more questions. For one, why doesn't the Gift work for Tristen and Mr. Jalisco?"

"It affects everyone differently," my mom says. "You and I, our cognitive functions were normal, and the Gift enhances that. With Tristen, it set out to do something else entirely. With his autism, his brain had too many synapses—"

"Wouldn't that be good?" I ask. "The more synapses a person has, the smarter they are."

"No, not exactly. As we develop, the brain teaches itself how to work. Part of that process is pruning synapses that don't provide healthy function. It can slow down the brain and jumble things up. The Gift rewired his brain and cured him of that, but it didn't make him any smarter."

"Thanks, Mom," Tristen said.

She blushes. "That came out wrong. You're plenty smart, as smart as anyone who doesn't have the Gift. All I'm saying is that flipping cars over with your mind or seeing into the future isn't...well, in your future."

"And Mr. Jalisco?" I ask.

"The Gift can only do so much before it would overwhelm a person. The dose I gave him was only strong enough to kill the tumor."

"Can't you just inject them again and give them the full Gift?"

"No, at least I don't think so. My guess is it would kill them. I'm certainly not going to find out."

"What about me?" I ask.

"The possibilities are endless. The bond that we share seems to bounce the effects back and forth between us. And since your brain is so much younger and more plastic, if your training goes as I hope I expect that you'll end up being the strongest person who's ever lived."

"And what happens then?"

"I can't say for sure."

"Can't you just look into the future and tell me?"

"I could, but that requires an extreme amount of energy and there's no time for that now. After I looked into the future to see when you would open the bond, I wasn't able to use the Gift for weeks and in that time we were captured."

"Wow, I'm sorry."

"Don't apologize," my dad says. "It wasn't your decision." He's holding my mom's hand and caressing her knuckles with his thumb. It's nice to see them together. I guess he was right to never stop loving her.

"How did you meet James?" I ask.

"After the incident at the lab, Tristen and I went into hiding. We ended up in the middle of Nebraska, in a small town called Hillbed. We were visiting the children in the hospital when we met him. He was also five years old, same as Tristen, and he was in a coma. An older boy in his orphanage had damaged his brain with a rock."

James reaches up feeling the scar that starts on his forehead and stretches up into his scalp.

"The doctors didn't think he would ever wake up from his coma. I used the Gift to get into his room and injected him with his own dose. It healed him but instead of enhancing his brain capabilities it locked them in. Nothing can get inside his head, no mind reading or control. I taught him to channel the energy and make it flow throughout his entire body. Now the powers of the Gift can't touch him at all if he doesn't want them to—no telekinesis or invisibility."

"And now the USI can do that too," Camden says.

We fall silent for a moment, considering this.

"So," I say, "the USI has learned how to block the Gift—not just mind control, but telekinesis too?"

"I believe so," my mom says.

"And what about you? By studying you, have they learned how to use the Gift like we do—not just block it?"

Her face is grim. "I suspect the USI has gained the ability to do everything we can, and the technology to stop us."

More silence.

"So do any of you have more questions?" my mom asks.

We shake our heads.

"Well, then tell us a little about life on the run?" my mom asks.

We spend the rest of the day bringing them up to date. I gloss over our time in USI detention, and though I consider skipping over what Camden did, I figure they deserve to know it all. My dad's face was as red as a brick when I was done with that part of the story, but he managed not to kill him. Besides, Camden's going to be a tool to get us back into the USI so I can't have him pretending that he doesn't know anything.

I end by insisting we rescue Em and Jackson. No one argues—which, if I'm going to be honest, is almost a little disappointing. I had this long motivational speech planned out.

We say our good nights to each other and crawl into bed. Finally I have my own room—no more awkward tension between the boys. Not to mention this is my first time in a bed since London—I almost forgot how amazing a proper mattress can feel.

∞   ∞   ∞

"Good morning."

I open my eyes to see my mother standing over me with a tray in her hands. Is this real? Am I actually getting breakfast in bed from my mom? Her smile shines through her eyes. I haven't seen someone so happy in months.

"Good morning," I say. "What's the special occasion?"

"The occasion is that this is the first time I've been able to be here when you woke up in the morning since you were two years old."

"Thank you." I say as she sets the tray down on my lap.

"You're welcome. Now eat your breakfast and get ready for the day. Training starts in thirty minutes."

I scarf—James did a good job dressing up his powdered eggs, but nothing beats the real thing. More than anything, I'm giddy to finally begin some real training.

Everyone is already up and training by the time I get outside. James, Tristen, and Camden were sparring. My mom and dad are off doing...actually, I can't tell what they're doing. I jump in with the boys until my mom comes back.

"Alright, Paris, you ready to get over your block?" she asks.

"I am. But I'm a little nervous too."

"Come with me," she says, leading me over the ridgeline and down the opposite slope until we're out of sight of the others.

"Okay so what's first?" I ask. "How do I get the Gift back?"

"Close your eyes. Whatever the USI used to temporarily block the Gift has worn off weeks ago."

"So what do—"

"Don't interrupt. Just listen for now and keep your eyes closed. I can feel the Gift is back and fully functional—you just have to overcome your fears...you're afraid that using the Gift might hurt someone. Afraid that you aren't strong enough to help Emily. Afraid that you are nothing without the Gift. You're afraid that if you get the Gift back you will still fail. But Paris, you are capable of so much more than you know. You have no limitations because you can do anything you set your mind to, with or without this Gift. The Gift is a tool, but a tool can only do so much. It's about how much you put into it. Visualize your fears. Choose a shape, a color—tie it to a balloon and let it go. Don't let your fears drag you down."

Okay. I breathe deeply, in and out, then let them go.

"Now visualize the block, maybe as a wall. Then watch as it crumbles to the ground."

"Mom," I say while opening my eyes.

"Yes?"

"I know you couldn't be around while I was growing up, but I wish you were."

My mom locks me in a bear hug. "I'm here now," she whispers in my ear, "and I'm never letting go." A hot tear drops onto my face, causing me to pull back.

"What now?" I ask.

"Clear your mind entirely. Nothing but empty space. Then picture what you want to do in your mind. Don't lose your focus. Here, take this necklace." She unclasps it from around her neck and places it in my hand. "Lift it."

I close my eyes and clear my mind. Only thinking about the necklace and how I want it to rise. I picture it lifting into the air and hovering inches above my hand. I open my eyes and nothing.

"Something's holding you back. What is it?"

"I don't know," I say.

"Paris, you can do this. I'm going to leave you be. It may take days to overcome this and it's better for you to practice on your own."

"Wait Mom!" I chase after her. "I did it once—I can do it again." I hold out the necklace and stare directly at it, demanding it to rise. The necklace shakes then lies still.

My mom takes the necklace and clasps it around my neck. "You're almost there. The wall is beginning to crumble. Keep working on it and have patience. Once you're ready come join the rest of us for a little one-on-one sparring."

"Thanks, Mom." I stroke the necklace, the first present my mom has given me. The necklace shakes in my hand and I let go. It rises up eye level. "Mom, are you doing this?"

"No. Congratulations, you're back!"

"I'm not. Who's doing this?"

"Guilty," a man says as he appears on the ridgeline.

"Ryker!" my mom says.

"Nikki, great job with the twenty-four hour Gift," he says. "It works wonderfully."

"How much longer do you have with it?" she asks.

"I used it yesterday to get back undetected, so only a couple more hours."

"You're the man from Mexico," I say. "You saved my life."

"I am." He tips an imaginary cap. "It's a pleasure to officially meet you."

"Paris, this is your Uncle Ryker," my mom says. "Your dad's brother."

"But Dad said you died when I was little."

"I didn't die, I was just lost for a while," Ryker says.

"Welcome back to the family, then," I say, going in for a hug.

"Thanks. I would love to stay and talk more but I'm going to go catch up with your dad and brother."

$$\infty \qquad \infty \qquad \infty$$

Day after day passes and I'm growing stronger. It's similar to what people say about riding a bike, how it's all muscle memory. I quickly catch back up to the level I was at before and then my mom takes over training.

I master more and more skills with the help of the bond. I can read and control minds, use telekinesis, turn myself and others invisible, hear from blocks away, send messages and energy to my mom, and steal energy from my surroundings in order to fight for longer periods of time. I'm working my butt off, training every second from the crack of dawn until well into the night, yet I still have a ways to go. But for now it's enough to break into the New Mexico base and rescue Em and Jackson.

While I'm busy training the boys are conjuring up a plan using Camden's knowledge of the base. After nearly four weeks we're fully rested, healed, and ready.

Extraction

THE DAY HAS FINALLY COME. It's been five weeks and I can't imagine how Em must be feeling. She must think we abandoned her, that we're never coming back and she'll be locked in that hell until they get bored and decide to kill her. She's not going to feel that way for much longer.

Camden's USI-issued black sedan is loaded, bags are packed, and plans finalized. Stripping the car of all its tracking mechanisms and electronics took some time, but it's now as electronically dumb as a 1920 Ford. I'm so anxious that I can't control myself any longer, and I begin pushing and pulling people into the car. Everyone but Ryker is coming—me, Tristen, James, Camden, Mom, and Dad. My mom mentioned something about Ryker searching for more recruits but at this point I just want everyone in the car so that we can go.

It's roughly a nine-hour drive. But my dad does it in seven. No need to worry about cops when you've got my mom and me. Just like before we sing, play games, talk, and sing some more. Although this car ride was a little more awkward than the last one because now I'm wedged in between James and Camden with Tristen sprawled out in the back. My dad insists that he'll drive the entire time.

"So Paris, once we get Em back the gang will finally be reunited," Camden says.

That almost makes me feel sorry for him. Because it's never going to be the same as it was in school. Too much has happened, too much has been lost. We're new people now, and if we're going to make it work, he'll have to take the risk of growing up and embracing what the future holds.

I catch my dad eyeing me in the rear-view mirror. With a smirk, he puts on "Let It Go" from the Frozen soundtrack. I blush, but then I remember what he told me more than once: "It's not awkward unless you make it awkward." He's right—I don't have to let this be awkward.

A couple hours before dawn, my dad pulls us off the road and drives across the desert until he finds a little rise to hide behind. He parks the car and we settle down to sleep. Both Camden and James have one hand lying on their thighs, palm up, ready for me to grab it. I look back and forth between the two. Whoever's hand I grab I'll end up sleeping on them, cuddling. I try to make a pros and cons list, and the outcome leans more toward Camden. Once I realize that, I am disappointed. My head is telling me Camden, but my heart is saying James.

I grab James's hand, swing his arm around me, and snuggle into him.

∞   ∞   ∞

James is shaking me awake. I slowly open my eyes into a squint and see him looking at me with the most amazing smile. We slide out of the car and join the rest of the group that had gathered on top of the hill. The sun was beginning to rise, warming my body from head to toe.

"So let's review the plan," my dad says. "Paris and Nikki are going to turn us invisible as we walk to the entrance. Then Camden will use his key card to get us in. Once we're in you four will go to the cells to rescue Em and Jackson while Nikki and I attempt to recover any additional information about the USI's plans. Camden, you lead the way to the cells."

"Why aren't we using your twenty-four hour injection of the Gift?" Tristen asks.

"Because we have a very limited supply and we can handle this without it," my mom says.

"Remember," my dad says, "this is only a rescue mission, so once you find Em and Jackson, get out of there immediately. Is everyone ready?"

We nod.

"Perfect. Let's move."

My mom and I look at each other and begin linking up. Once everyone is invisible we begin our trek down the hill.

It takes about nine minutes to reach the windowless grey box they call a base, and it's already a struggle for me to walk. Maintaining my group's invisibility is exhausting.

Camden swipes his key card to the base, opening the side door. It's exactly how I remember it. Dark walls, bland and boring. No color anywhere. Narrow hallways leading off at seemingly random angles. The black floors sparkle in the light's reflection.

My mom and dad split off—I hope they know where they're going. I guess my dad still remembers his way around after working here all those years ago.

Camden leads us down a hallway to our left toward the cells. We take a right, then another right, then hurry down a flight of stairs. We turn left, left again, then right, and then I drop to my knees, breaking the link and revealing everyone.

Em is lying on the floor of her cell, scarred and bruised. Tears stream down my face. How could I let this happen to my best friend? She has been there for me ever since we met, and this is what she gets in return?

After a moment I realize that she's not alone. A beautiful girl about our age with light brown hair is sitting in the corner.

I rip the cell door off its hinges and set it against the wall. Em's face lights up with excitement when she sees me, but after a moment her expression turns to fear and she scrambles backward until she's pressed against the wall.

"Who are you?" she asks.

"What? It's me, Paris."

"I'm not falling for this again. Who are you?"

"Em, I promise it's me."

"Prove it."

"Almost every day for months we used to visit Bentley in the hospital before she passed away from leukemia."

"Anyone could know that," she says. "What was the last thing she said to us?"

"She made us promise to always have courage and be kind. And to help others do the same."

"Paris!" Em stands up and dives into my arms.

"We have to move," I say. "We don't have much time."

Em nods and lets go of me. Tristen puts his arm around her—he's crying too—and helps her out of the cell.

"Come on, Avery," Em says. "We're getting out of here."

The other girl follows us into the hallway. It looks like she hasn't seen the sun in five years.

"Where's Jackson?" Camden asks.

"I can take you," Avery says.

"Please," I say, motioning for her to lead the way. The six of us link up and I turn us all invisible. I almost faint—it's like someone is sucking the blood out of me with a fire hose.

Avery leads us back upstairs. From time to time we press against the wall to let an agent pass, though the hallways are mostly empty at this hour. We turn down a hallway painted a bright yellow with sky blue trim that's decorated with children's drawings of race cars, dinosaurs, and flowers.

"What is this place?" I ask.

"It's the children's wing," Avery says. Jackson and I grew up here."

At the end of the hall there are two doors. Avery opens up the one on the left. A little boy lies asleep on his bed. The carpet is covered in toys, and there's a TV in the corner.

I make Camden visible, and he rushes to Jackson's side. "Hey dude," he whispers. "We're going to go somewhere new."

Jackson reaches up and wraps his skinny arms around Camden's neck. My heart melts. Jackson looks almost exactly like his older brother.

"Let's go," I say. "Camden, you lead the way." I turn him invisible again, along with his brother. The seven of us link hands and hurry toward the exit. After several turns Camden backs up around the corner and the rest of us bump into each other one by one.

"The exit is guarded," Camden whispers. "There's two of them."

Mom, can you hear me? I ask.

Yes. Did you find Em and Jackson?

Yes, and another girl named Avery. But the door is guarded. We need to take them out.

Wait for us before you do anything.

A minute or two later my parents arrive in the hallway.

"So what's the plan?" I ask my mom after making our group visible.

"I'll take care of the guards," my dad says. "Camden, you open the doors. Then we run."

My mom and I turn everyone invisible again. A moment later the two guards' heads slam together and they fall unconscious. Camden swipes his key card, triggering sirens instead of opening the door.

"They know we're here," he says. "Get ready—we're gonna have a lot of company real quick."

My mom unlinks, revealing everyone. "It looks like we're going to have to fight our way out of here after all," she says.

"Paris, break that door down," my dad says.

"I don't think I can."

"You have to. We don't have enough ammunition to hold them off for longer than a couple of minutes."

"Camden, any ideas?" I ask.

"Hit it with everything you've got."

Great. Okay, what first? Using telekinesis I search the inside of the door for any kind of switch I can trigger. Nope, there's nothing but a big block of steel. I press my hand against the door, close my eyes, and push while imagining my hand going through the door. I feel a warm breeze on my fingertips.

Shots fire behind me. They're here. I need to be faster.

I wonder…no, I don't think it's possible. Well, maybe. It can't hurt to try. I close my eyes, visualizing all the energy surging through my body and sending it into the palms of my hands. I push the door as hard as I can, using the energy as an extension of my strength. I drop to the floor, too weak to stand. I have no strength, no energy left, and nothing to draw from to refurbish my energy.

The door cracked, and the sunlight coming from outside illuminates the damage like a glowing spider web. One more hit like that and the door might open. But it's going to take me some time before I have enough energy to do that again.

I rest my back against the door and watch the scene in front of me. My mom is standing opposite the intersection between our hallway and the one running diagonally through ours. She's using the Gift to create some kind of shield to block the agents' gunfire. Camden, Tristen, James, and my dad are crouched behind the four corners of the intersection and returning fire when they can.

"Paris, get that door open!" my dad shouts.

"I need more time!" I shout back.

"We don't have more time! There's at least fifty agents out here and we're running out of ammo!"

I wobble back to my feet and face the door. I close my eyes and slow my heart rate. Then I release all my energy with one giant push, and the door falls backward, kicking up a huge cloud of dust as it lands with a crash.

"Camden!" I shout. "Go get the car and come pick us up!"

Camden grabs Jackson's arm and takes off toward the car.

I turn around to see a USI agent grappling with James's gun. Avery lays down fire from the opposite corner but three more agents rush through the gap of suppressive fire. Avery pulls out a knife and slices the upper thigh of one, then spins around and slashes a second agent's wrist as he aims his gun at me. She catches the gun in midair and shoots the third agent and then the one fighting for James's gun.

"Avery!" Someone shouts from out of view. I recognize that voice. Terrence.

"Avery, it's okay," Terrence says. "You didn't know what you were doing. I can help you."

"Avery," Em says. "Avery, look at me."

Avery whips around. She looks confused and scared.

"You'll be safe with us, I promise you." Em touches Avery's shoulder. "You trust me, right?"

"I..." Avery begins.

"Avery, are you really going to listen to some girl you just met instead of your father? We're family—does that mean nothing to you?"

A car honks behind me. Camden's back.

"Let's go!" I shout.

I watch a tear leave Avery's eye as she runs toward the car with Em.

Tristen, James, and my dad lay down cover fire as my mom retreats through the intersection with her shield still up. Tristen and my dad open up with their guns and then dive across the intersection while James fires from his post. The three men follow me into the car while my mom stands just outside the door, protecting us with her shield.

"Hit the gas!" my dad shouts when my mom gets into the car. Shots fire at the back window, kicking up white starbursts as the rounds strike the bulletproof glass.

We rumble across the desert for about five minutes before my dad tells Camden to stop. He and my mom get into the driver and passenger seats while Camden and Jackson join Tristen and Avery in the middle. James, Em, and I are in the back.

"We should be good," my dad says as we start driving.

"Why is no one chasing after us?" I ask.

"Jack and Wyatt took care of all their cars. Is everyone okay?"

"I think we're all good." Tristen says.

I glance up at James. His lips are cut and his nose is bleeding but he still looks like an angel. He puts his arm around me as I lie on his shoulder. Em squeezes my hand then rests her head on me.

My dad drives back to the cabin while the rest of us sleep. Those seven hours pass by extremely fast and before we know it, my dad is giving us the fifteen-minute warning.

"Avery, why did your dad put you in that cell with Em?" I ask.

"I heard that a girl was being held there, so I went to visit her. Emily and I became fast friends. I was just hanging out with her when you guys showed up."

"So if you weren't a prisoner then why did you come with us?" I ask.

"I was a prisoner," Avery says. "I spent my entire life locked up in that base. I rarely ever saw my dad. It was just me and Jackson."

"I don't understand how someone doesn't love their own child," I say.

"He does love me," Avery protests.

"Well, then he has an interesting way of showing it," Camden says.

"Terrence wasn't always like this," my dad says. "He used to be one of the bravest men I know. Always looking out for the little guy. An amazing commander."

"He was nicer to us than everyone else," Jackson says.

"What happened to him?" Camden asks.

"Me," Avery says. "My mom passed away during her C-section."

"Avery, I—"

"He resents me for it," she says, cutting me off. "She was the only person he really cared for, and she kept him human. After she died, he had no one."

"Avery," my dad begins, "I know Terrence loves you. He just—"

"He just sees her in me every time he looks at me. I know, I've heard it before. But losing my mom broke him and whoever put him back together did it wrong."

"Why did you come with us?" I ask again. As sorry as I feel for her, we can't have someone with us for the wrong reasons.

"Deep down I believe there's a better man. But he can't continue like this. Hurting innocent people just isn't right. I'll do whatever it takes to either stop him or help him realize the right way. Besides, Jackson's like my little brother, I wasn't going to leave him."

Em reaches over the seat and grabs Avery's hand. "If it wasn't for Avery, I don't think I would have made it through —"

Em's eyes roll to the back of her head as she begins to seize.

"What's happening?" I shout.

"Uh, I don't know." Avery says.

"Well, think!"

"Um…it could be my father's formula for the Gift," Avery says. "He's been trying to replicate it for years. A doctor injected her with something last night." Tears form in her eyes. "I'm so sorry."

"This is how it's supposed to start," my mom says.

"And then?" I ask.

"Then, um, then you either wake up, or you don't."

Silence follows. Once we arrive at the cabin, Tristen, James, and my dad carry Em inside and lay her on my bed. I ask everyone else to leave. I sit with her, holding her hand as she continues to convulse.

"Em, please, please wake up. I can't..." Tears stream down my face. "I can't lose you again. Please wake up. You're the best friend I've ever had."

Memories of our best times together flood in. The time we first met in English class. Our first sleepover—Em laughed so hard that milk came out her nose. When we would go shopping and force each other to put on the worst dresses imaginable. The first day of senior year, when my dress got caught on my backpack—I walked down the halls with my underwear showing—Em still teases me about that.

Em's body finally falls still. I jerk up. "Em! Emily, can you hear me?"

No response.

"Mom, she stopped shaking!"

My mom walks into the room and peels back Em's eyelids. Em stares up at the ceiling, unseeing.

"Mom, what happens next? How long till she wakes up?"

"It should happen immediately after she stops seizing." She touches my shoulder and I twist away.

"She's going to wake up. The USI's formula just works differently."

"Paris..."

"No, she's going to wake up, you'll see. Any second now."

A minute passes, and then another. My mom takes Em's wrist and feels for a pulse. "Paris…"

"No!!" I shout. Windows shatter and paint chips fall from the ceiling as a flood of rage pours out of my body.

Em's dead.

We failed her.

Time Is the Measure of Change

I SPEND THE NEXT WEEK lying in bed, in the same bed that Em died in. My dad forces me to eat twice a day, but otherwise I don't see anyone. I won't even go to the bathroom unless they're all outside training. James, Tristen, and my mom all try to visit me, but I keep my door locked and refuse to answer when they knock.

"Paris, it's Camden. Can I come in?"

"Go away."

"Paris, please. I can't imagine what this must feel like, but I do know that it's going to be even harder to face alone. I loved her too, you know."

"You loved her? You left her there to die when you rescued me."

"You're right. I made the wrong choice and I'm going to have to live with that for the rest of my life."

"Oh, shut up. I don't want to hear it."

Camden doesn't respond, and after a minute I realize he has simply walked away. I feel a flash of anger—I want to yell at him some more, blame him for Em's death.

What am I saying? It's not his fault—he risked his life to save mine, and James and Tristen's. And he risked his life a second time to go back for her. I'm blaming him because I feel guilty. They hurt Em to get to me.

So then shouldn't I be blaming my mom for all of this? She's the one who infected me with the Gift when I was just two years old. Of course not. None of us are to blame for this. This all falls on Terrence and the USI.

I get out of bed and walk to the kitchen.

"I know, I just don't know how," my dad says.

"Maybe she needs more time," my mom says.

"She doesn't need more time, she needs our love and support."

"You're right," I say, "It's not healthy and I'm not going to get any better in there. But for a while I didn't want to get better. And now, I'm not sure, but I'm sick of feeling like this."

"Paris!" James exclaims.

"Paris, would you like some lunch?" my mom asks. "You must be starving."

"Yeah, food sounds good. What is there?"

"Orange chicken with rice and broccoli."

I sit down at the table and start eating. I feel like everyone's staring at me so I keep my head down and concentrate on swallowing. With my shrunken stomach it's hard to do.

"So Avery and I have been talking," my mom says, "and we feel like it's best to act quickly."

"Act how?" I ask.

"Taking out Terrence and the USI, of course."

I feel a red flash of rage at the sound of Terence's name. The window behind my mom explodes, showering us with glass. Startled, I jump back from the table and accidentally slide it across the room, smashing Avery and James into the wall.

"I'm so sorry!" I run back to my room, lock the door, curl up in a ball on the bed, and begin to cry.

"Please let me in," my mom whispers through the door.

I don't answer, but a locked door is no problem for my mom. She crawls into bed with me.

"I didn't mean to," I sob.

"I know, everyone knows. You would never do something like that on purpose."

"I haven't been able to control it since, since…I break everything I touch."

Instead of answering, my mom just holds me as I cry.

"Is there any way to go back?" I ask.

"Go back? You mean go back in time?"

"Yes."

"Oh, sweetie, I'm so sorry, but I don't think there's a way. At least I haven't found one."

"Have you ever tried?"

"Well, not really."

"So there could be a way. If we work together we could figure it out. Will you help me find a way?"

"Paris I don't think it's a good idea."

"Mom, please. I can't not try. I have to at least try and bring her back or I'm never going to be able to move on. Not if I knew there was something I could have done."

"I want to help you, but I really don't think—"

"Get out!" I shriek. The force of my anger sends my mom flying across the room and into the wall. Plaster falls from the ceiling.

"I'm so sorry, I didn't mean to," I sob.

My dad runs into the room. "Nikki, are you okay?" He asks, helping her up. "Paris, I know you're going through a hard time, but you need to get control of yourself. Is this really how you think Emily would have wanted you to represent her memory? Holed up in your room, giving up on living? She would be furious. Focus on all the good times you had together, and don't let Terrence win."

I'm too stunned to answer. No one has talked to me like that since Em died. They've been handling me with kid gloves, and maybe that's made it worse. Or maybe he was just lashing out at me, furious that I'd hurt my mom. Not that I didn't deserve it. Now I'm crying so hard it feels like I'm going to pass out.

"Paris!" It's Jackson. "We need your help!"

"Get out," I moan. "I don't want to hurt you."

"Please, James and Camden are fighting. They're going to get hurt."

I sit up and look out the window. James is on top of Camden and punching him in the face while Camden is fighting back with punches to James's ribs. I rush out of the room and out of the house.

"What are you guys doing?" I shout.

The two of them freeze. James quickly gets off of Camden and both of them stand up.

"We were—" James begins.

"We were just talking about you," Camden interrupts.

"Me? Why on earth would that lead to this?"

"Paris, there has been enough games," James says. "You need to choose between the two of us." He reaches out to take my hand and I jump back.

"Don't touch me!" I shout. I trip on a rock and fall backward into the dirt. "Stay back."

"Paris, it's okay," Camden says, walking toward me.

"No, stay back!" I shout, and the two of them go flying ten feet back and skid across the ground, their bodies throwing up columns of dust.

"I told you to stay back. I can't control it." I'm crying again.

James wobbles to his feet and walks straight for me. I shake my head, but he keeps walking. Before I can tell him to go away, he is crouching at my side, holding me in his arms.

"Paris, you're not hurting me. I'm okay, you're okay, everyone's okay. You can calm down."

"I can't control it."

"I know. Somehow when you exploded you unlocked more power or whatever it is inside you. It's going to take some time until you can control the Gift again."

Camden crouches down on my other side. "You don't have to do this alone. We're all here for you. Let us help."

"Paris, we want to be here for you," James says. "We'll always be here for you no matter what."

"I can't believe you are asking me to choose. After all that's happened."

"Paris, please. Just tell us." Camden says.

"I can't lose either of you."

"You won't," he says, and James nods.

I look at James, and then Camden. I've already made my decision—now I just have to find the words. "I don't know how."

"How to choose?" James asks.

"No, how to tell you, to put words to my feelings. I don't know how to be sure I won't lose you."

"Who can't you lose?" Camden asks. "Who do you love, Paris?"

"Love? I'm eighteen years old, I don't know what love feels like."

"Yes, you do. We were in love—that's what love feels like. What we had, it was real."

"No, what we had was a child's love, Camden. A love we were capable of at the time. Every day I'm getting older, I'm growing up, I'm experiencing new things. And I'm still only eighteen. I have such a long way to go."

"Why can't you open your heart?" Camden pleads. "Let your childish love—if that's what you want to call it—let it grow and mature with you. Love is beautiful and amazing —don't shut it out."

"No, love lost when Em died."

Neither of them knows what to say to that.

"Dinner's ready," Avery calls out from behind me. I stand up and brush the dust off my clothes.

"Paris, can I have a moment with you alone?" Camden asks.

I shrug and stand there like a sleepwalker while James sulks away toward the house.

"Paris, before you shut the door on love, please reconsider. Do you remember what I said to you after New Mexico?"

"You said…"

"I promised that I would never stop fighting for you. For your trust, your love, for you. I love you and I will be here for you always. I will wait as long as I have to until I can get you back because I promised."

"Camden, don't," I whisper.

"I promised."

"I can't love. Not anymore. Not right now."

"Yes you can. Let me back into your heart. I know you still have feelings for me. Stop shutting them out. Give us another chance."

I shake my head.

"Not a day goes by where I don't wish that I could go back and say something, do something different, but I can't. I screwed up. I screwed up big time. I know I did. All I'm asking for is another chance to prove to you how much you mean to me."

A tear slides down my cheek. "I don't want you to prove anything to me. I want you to be my friend. Not my boyfriend."

"And I will, but I will never stop fighting to become something more because I promised you."

"Do you remember what I said to you?" I ask.

"What?"

"Do you remember what I said to you after New Mexico? I said I would always love you, but not in the same way that you love me. I can't. Every time I look at you all I can see is you trying to cuff me. That's what I said, and it's true. When you turned on me, you changed me. For better or for worse, I don't know yet. All I know is I'm different now. Now I know it was a childish love."

"But it wasn't."

"It was for me. Camden, I don't want you to wait. I want you to move on. I'm letting you out of your promise. I'm letting you go."

"No, I won't. I don't want to."

"I hope you'll find someone who can love you the same way you love me. But that person is not me."

Camden turns and walks away.

"Camden! Wait, please." I run after him and grab his hand, pulling him back around to face me. "Please I can't lose you." Camden shakes his arm free. I throw my arms around his neck and pull him in for a kiss. Memories of all the good times we had flood back. Camden wraps his arm around my waist, pulling me in closer.

I step away, wiping at my tears with the back of my hand. "I'm sorry, I just needed—"

"I know," Camden says.

"So we're—"

"For now. For now, friends."

I smile and we walk inside to join the others.

"Paris, how are you feeling?" my dad asks nervous.

"Thank you, Dad. I really needed to hear that. I'm not sure how long it will take, but I think at some point I'll be okay."

He engulfs me in a bear hug.

"No!" I shout. He drops to the ground, wincing in pain and starting to convulse. "I'm sorry, I can't control it."

"Paris, stop!" my mom shouts.

"I'm trying," I say. "I don't know how."

"Paris, focus on me. Focus on my voice. You can do this. Just visualize the energy like I taught you. Visualize it and stop sending it. Your overloading his system with energy, he can't take it."

"Okay." I close my eyes and focus. I see the energy pulsing from my body to my dad's and I sever the tie.

"Mom, what's happening to me?"

"When Emily passed, you lost control and in the process you fully accepted the Gift. It's as if you were testing the waters, seeing if you liked how it felt, and now you dove in and you're freezing."

"She can get control of this, right?" James asks. "And it won't hurt her?"

"I'm not sure," my mom says. "I think so. But this is all new."

"Well, that's enough talk about the Gift for now," my dad says as he slowly picks himself up off the floor. "The food's getting cold."

"Yes, thank you Dad," Tristen says. "It smells delicious."

Everyone takes turns fixing a plate of chicken, mashed potatoes, salad, and fruit before taking a seat at the long dinner table next to the kitchen. We pause to say grace before eating.

"So I know I have missed a lot," I say. "Maybe you guys could bring me up to speed on taking down Terrence."

"Are you sure?" Avery asks. "We don't have to talk about it right now if you don't want to."

"I'm sure. I want to stay in the loop."

"Okay," my mom says. "Avery and I have been strategizing about the best plan of attack. We've come up with a couple options, but we're not sure which one is right just yet."

"What's the best plan so far?" I ask.

"I've sent Ryker to recruit as many people as possible who have been injected and trained with the Gift."

"Wait, I didn't know other people have the Gift," Jackson says.

"Not many, but through the years I gave it to those whom I trusted or those in need of it."

"So this plan?" I ask.

"Right. Ryker is visiting one last person and then we should be ready. About two months ago Ryker stole information from the USI database. They're close to replicating my formula. Within a couple weeks close. In exactly one week Terrence will be meeting with the board of the USI to make his case for the approval of his plan."

"And his plans are what exactly?" I ask.

"To inject all of his agents, creating an unstoppable army of super soldiers. If he succeeds in creating his army there's nothing left we can do. Our best hope is to crash the board meeting and prove to them Terrence is unstable and corrupt."

"And if we can't?" I ask.

"We go to Plan B: switch his formula with my temporary formula and pray we have recruited enough people to put an end to him. We do have a secret weapon—Avery. He won't hurt her, so she can get close to him."

"Avery, are you sure?" Tristen asks.

"Whatever it takes," Avery says with a shockingly adult look. Tristen looks away.

"Paris, can I talk to you privately?" my mom asks. She stands up from the table and I follow her into my room.

"How are you?" she asks.

"I'm overwhelmed. I don't know what to think. I don't want to think."

"Can I ask a favor of you?"

"Anything."

"I need you to look into the future," she says. "I'm not strong enough."

"The future? Why?"

"I need to know if this is the right plan. We can't let Terrence succeed."

"I don't know how," I say.

"I'll teach you."

"Okay. When do we start?"

"How about right now?"

A cold wave of fear washes through me.

"You can do this," my mom says. "I've only been able to do this twice, and both times were by accident. But you're much stronger than I am. I think you can choose a precise moment in the future to look at."

"How?"

"Well, when I did it I was practicing a different skill. I was trying to slow time, or at least that's how I describe it. It's how I 'teleport.' It takes an enormous amount of energy so I can only hold it for a short while, although I think you would be able to hold it for much, much longer."

"How do I do it?"

"You start with calming your entire body. Take a couple of long deep breaths then choose an object or person and observe everything. I used a clock my first time. Listen to the sound of the hour, minute, and second hand. Once you can hear it very clearly, you focus in on the second hand and watch as it goes around. Try to slow the hand down as it goes around the clock. Turn one second into two, then three, then four, until a second is five minutes, or ten. But don't be disappointed if you can't do it right away —it took me a year to master this skill."

"And we only have a week."

"You can do it, Paris. Just practice."

"And what do I do after I slow everything down?" I ask.

"I don't know. Remember, it was an accident. But I have faith you'll figure it out."

"Well, that's helpful," I mutter.

My mom walks out of the room.

"Okay, focus. You can do this," I say to myself. I stare down at the clock, which is now cracked and lying on the floor, and listen for the clicking noise as the hands move. After a couple of minutes I smile—I can hear it. Click, click, click.

Onto slowing it down. I stare at the clock for hours, trying and failing to get the second hand to slow. Finally I give up and go to bed.

After breakfast the following morning, I return to my room and get back to work. I skip lunch and then dinner but make no progress. It seems like I should be frustrated but it's almost like I'm meditating—my first escape from the grief of Em's passing since she died.

By the third day I can slow the second hand down to where it clicks every couple of minutes, but I still have no idea how to look into the future.

On the fifth day I can make a second last a full ten minutes. I suppress my excitement and focus even deeper. I open my eyes to see the clock has stopped completely. I run out of the room to see if everyone else is frozen. My mom is standing at the kitchen sink. The water flowing from the tap is suspended in mid-air. James is sitting at the table, holding a sandwich halfway to his mouth. I wave my hand in front of his unseeing eyes.

∞ ∞ ∞

Run, my mom says.

I break out into a sprint, unsure of what I'm running from.

Turn left.

Faster.

Turn right.

Faster.

"No!" I shout as I pound the wall in front of me, a dead end in the maze of the USI base. "No," I whisper. Fear settles as an ominous laugh echoes behind me.

"It's over. You lost."

"No." I whisper, my back now pressed against the wall. I slide to the ground, clutching my hair with my knees pulled up into my chest. "Please."

"You're a threat and I can't risk it."

Terrence strides toward me, sending a shot of fear into my heart with each step. I try to stop him with the Gift, but nothing works. I look down, engulfed in pain. Blood is everywhere. There's nothing more I can do. He's right—I lost.

Cries for help echo through the dark halls followed by gunshots. The cold tip of his knife inches closer, ready to strike.

I stand up and begin to run. Run anywhere but here. As I reach the end of the hall I stop—the pain is gone somehow. I turn around to see my body drop, helpless, breathless, lifeless.

∞   ∞   ∞

I gasp as I snap back to reality. "He wins," I say to my mom.

Paris!

She turns around, startled by my sudden presence. "How does he win?"

"I don't know. But he kills me. I saw myself die."

Paris!

"Did you hear that?" I ask.

"Yes, he kills you. But that's not the end of this. We'll figure out something else."

Paris!

"There it is again," I say.

"You die, but are you sure he wins?" my mom asks.

"I heard people screaming. And Terrence said, 'It's over. You lost.' Then he started laughing."

Paris!

The voice is so loud that I have to cover my ears. "Are you sure you're not hearing this?"

"Focus. Is there anything else you remember? Anything that can help us come up with a new plan?"

Paris!

"No. I'm sorry."

Paris!

My mom says something else but no sound comes out. Her body starts to fade. I grab at her arm but my hand passes right through her.

Paris!

"What's happening to me?"

∞   ∞   ∞

I wake up and see a bright light shining down on me. There's a steady beeping sound to my left.

"What happened?" I ask.

"You passed out," Em said. "I told the doctors you were out hunting and you tripped and shot yourself. I know it's not a great story, but it was hard to come up with something on the spot. Oh, and I gave them a fake name in case someone here worked for the USI."

"Em?"

"Yes?"

"How is this happening? You're dead."

"What are you talking about?"

"I watched you die."

"Par, you're not thinking straight. The nurse hooked you up to an IV. She said she was giving you some pain meds and something to help you sleep since that was the best way to recover."

"This doesn't make any sense," I say.

"I think it's time for you to explain what happened," Em says. "Is this why you were out of school for so long?"

"What? You know what happened."

"No. I know you got shot and then you lifted a man with your mind. What's going on?"

"Is this real?" I ask.

"Yes, of course this is real," Camden says. "What's going on?"

"This is real?" I say with tears in my eyes. "You're alive." I reach up and hug Em, ignoring the flare of pain in my shoulder.

"Paris, take it easy" Em says.

"I can't believe you're alive. I can save you. You don't have to die. We don't have to lose."

Epilogue

EM GRABS MY ARM and pulls me to a stop. "Paris, why are we doing this?"

"My mom's in London," I say, rushing toward our gate. Our flight leaves in twenty minutes.

"And why can't Camden come with us?"

"He works for the USI."

"What? How do you know all of this?"

"I'll explain on the plane but we have to hurry." I reach out for her hand. "Please Em, trust me."

Her lip quivers. "Okay."

Together we make our way to our gate. A Delta flight from SLC to Atlanta, then Boston, then finally London. The best I could do on such short notice.

The line dwindles and soon it's our turn to board. "Par, we don't have tickets." Em says, tugging at my arm to go back.

"Ticket please," the attendant says.

Let us through.

"Enjoy your flight," she says, gesturing us aboard.

"How do you keep doing that?" Em whispers to me.

"I learned to in a dream." At least I think it was a dream of the future. It could be that this is my second chance at the past, but either way it felt real. Real enough that I remember it all. All the training. All the torture. And James. All of James.

"The dream where I die?"

"Yes, but I'm not going to let that happen."

"Paris, you should be in the hospital. If you keep moving your arm you're going to rip those stitches."

"I'm fine, Mom," I say, mocking her. We find two empty seats in first class. "Déjà vu."

"Huh?"

"Right, you don't remember." Will no one remember? Camden sacrificing everything to save us. Ryker becoming Ryker again. My dad and Mom reuniting. Tristen and Em falling in love. James and me.

James and me. Will he not remember either? Will he not remember me?

"Okay," Em says taking a deep breath. "I'm on the plane with you. Can you please explain now?"

I sigh. "I grew up believing that when I was three years old my mother walked out the door and never looked back. Recently, I learned that was a lie."

My seat rattles and my eye catches a man in a bright orange vest waving a blinking light. I feel a kick as the plane inches forward.

ABOUT THE AUTHOR

T. C. Steuer was in the eighth grade when she began writing. What started as a simple class assignment turned into a passion and after five years of discovery and development she's turned that passion into her first Novel. This bright, young talented girl set out to publish prior to graduating from high school and has proven that with hard work and determination, dreams are created. In celebration of her 18th birthday, T.C. Steuer manifested her dream and published the first Novel of the Infinite Series. Her authenticity and creative flare will delight all readers and surely produce many more books to come. T. C. Steuer will continue her studies at Brigham Young University.

www.ingramcontent.com/pod-product-compliance
Lightning Source LLC
Chambersburg PA
CBHW021235250626
47155CB00008B/3027